"Tell me why this is a bad idea," Dallas said.

He slid his hand around the back of Joelle's neck, angling her head. Angling her body, too, with the grip he still had on her waist. They were pressed against each other like lovers now.

"Because you can't forgive me?" she managed. "Because you hate me?"

He was right in her face, and she saw that register in his eyes. Both valid reasons. Well, the first one anyway. That didn't look like hate in all those swirls of blue in his eyes. No hate in his body, either. His breath was uneven. Heart racing.

"Because we don't have time for this." Joelle tried again. "And because you'd regret it."

Dallas kept staring for what seemed an eternity, and even though he didn't move, her body seemed to think it was about to get lucky with Dallas. Everything inside her was melting, urging her to do what Dallas had so far resisted.

Like kiss him…

USA TODAY Bestselling Author

DELORES FOSSEN

THE MARSHAL'S HOSTAGE

WITHDRAWN

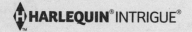

ISBN-13: 978-0-373-69686-4

THE MARSHAL'S HOSTAGE OCT 2 4 2013

HARLEQUIN®
www.Harlequin.com

Printed in U.S.A.

ABOUT THE AUTHOR

Imagine a family tree that includes Texas cowboys, Choctaw and Cherokee Indians, a Louisiana pirate and a Scottish rebel who battled side by side with William Wallace. With ancestors like that, it's easy to understand why *USA TODAY* bestselling author and former air force captain Delores Fossen feels as if she were genetically predisposed to writing romances. Along the way to fulfilling her DNA destiny, Delores married an air force top gun who just happens to be of Viking descent. With all those romantic bases covered, she doesn't have to look too far for inspiration.

Books by Delores Fossen

HARLEQUIN INTRIGUE
1091—SECURITY BLANKET**
1110—BRANDED BY THE SHERIFF‡
1116—EXPECTING TROUBLE‡
1122—SECRET DELIVERY‡
1144—SHE'S POSITIVE
1163—CHRISTMAS GUARDIAN**
1186—SHOTGUN SHERIFF
1205—THE BABY'S GUARDIAN‡‡
1211—DADDY DEVASTATING‡‡
1217—THE MOMMY MYSTERY‡‡
1242—SAVIOR IN THE SADDLE†
1248—WILD STALLION†
1252—THE TEXAS LAWMAN'S LAST STAND†
1269—GI COWBOY
1314—GRAYSON††
1319—DADE††
1324—NATE††
1360—KADE††
1365—GAGE††
1371—MASON††
1389—CHRISTMAS RESCUE AT MUSTANG RIDGE
1395—STANDOFF AT MUSTANG RIDGE
1419—THE MARSHAL'S HOSTAGE***

**Texas Paternity
‡Texas Paternity: Boots and Booties
‡‡Texas Maternity: Hostages
†Texas Maternity: Labor and Delivery
††The Lawmen of Silver Creek Ranch
***The Marshals of Maverick County

CAST OF CHARACTERS

Marshal Dallas Walker—He was raised in the notorious Rocky Creek orphanage, and the past he'd rather forget comes crashing back when his old flame is assigned to investigate a murder that could ultimately send him or his foster father to jail. Dallas has to walk a fine line between the law, family duty and a woman he just can't get out of his mind.

Joelle Tate—She, too, was brought up at Rocky Creek, and even though she's fighting the old attraction with Dallas, she also has secrets that put them on a collision course with not just the past but with new danger.

Kirby Granger—Sixteen years ago this now retired marshal rescued Dallas and five other boys from Rocky Creek, but he might have cut corners to do that.

Sarah Webb—The widow of the tyrannical headmaster at Rocky Creek. She could know more about her husband Jonah's murder than she's saying.

Owen Palmer—He and Dallas and Joelle have a shared past that wasn't always pleasant, and now he seems to be willing to do anything to make Joelle his wife.

Lindsey Downing—Owen's assistant, who is jealous of Joelle. But is she behind the attempts to kill Joelle and Dallas?

Rudy Simmons—The crusty groundskeeper at Rocky Creek. He claims he knows nothing about the headmaster's murder, but Dallas and Joelle aren't so sure.

Chapter One

Marshal Dallas Walker studied the three men milling around in front of the Maverick Springs church. All were dressed in nondescript black suits, but judging from the bulges beneath their coats, they were carrying weapons.

So, what were armed guests doing at a wedding?

Joelle's wedding.

Just thinking those two words put a knot in his gut, and seeing those armed men only made the knot even tighter.

Something wasn't right here—on many levels.

Dallas eased his hand over the Glock .22 in his holster and walked up the limestone path that led to the front door. As expected, he got the attention of all three men. They snapped toward him, and one whispered something into the communicator that he had strapped to his wrist.

The biggest one, a bald guy with linebacker-size shoulders, stepped forward to block Dallas's way. "Are you a guest of the bride or groom?" he asked, none too friendly.

Dallas debated his answer for a split second and decided to go with what would get him inside the church the fastest and with the least amount of trouble.

If that was possible.

He tapped his badge, which was clipped to his belt. "I'm Marshal Dallas Walker. Move or I'll move you."

Yeah, it wasn't very friendly, either, but at least he'd

given them an option. Of sorts. One way or the other, they were moving.

The man's jaw turned to iron, and he glanced at the one with the communicator. That one lifted his wrist and was about to say something into the device, probably something that would cause an ugly confrontation with these goons and the groom. But the squeaky sound and movement behind them had them all reaching for their weapons.

False alarm.

The sound was coming from a window being lifted in the century-old church. And there she was.

Joelle.

She looked out at him from behind the mesh window screen. No wedding dress, but she was wearing a white robe, and the April breeze took a swipe at the dark blond hair she had piled on her head. She gave all of them a glare.

Especially Dallas.

"What are *you* doing here?" she snapped.

"Seeing *you*," Dallas snapped right back.

And for good measure, he returned the glare, too. It wasn't hard to do. Once, when he was seventeen and stupid, he'd been in love with Joelle Tate, but it sure wasn't love he was feeling right now.

Far from it.

He wanted to wring her neck.

"We have to talk," Dallas insisted, and he elbowed his way through the trio of guards and hurried up the church steps.

He was on borrowed time now because it wouldn't be long before the groom, Owen Palmer, found out he was there, and Owen would not be a happy buckaroo about Dallas's arrival.

Get in line.

A lot of people wouldn't be happy about this little visit, but by God, he was not going to let Joelle get away with this.

Since his foster father, Kirby Granger, had brought Dallas and his brothers to this church plenty of times, Dallas knew the way through the mazelike corridors to the side room where Joelle was. He found her, all right. Waiting for him in the doorway.

And she was still glaring.

"Owen and I are getting married in an hour," Joelle informed him.

That sentence sounded as unright to him as the armed guards and the big fat diamond ring on her finger, but the wedding wasn't the reason for his visit. Nope. If Joelle had fallen in love with a weasel like Owen, then they deserved each other. Dallas had written her out of his life ages ago.

He took her by the arm and moved her back into the room. "We'll talk fast."

That definitely didn't help her glare. "Owen will be here soon."

"Then we'll talk *faster*."

There were two women in the room, both wearing flowing yellow dresses, and he figured they were Joelle's friends from Austin, where she'd lived for the past four years or so. One of them was holding a big puffy wad of silk and lace.

The wedding dress, no doubt.

Dallas turned to the women and hitched his thumb to the door. "I need to talk to Joelle alone." And yeah, he added some attitude to that *request* because he wasn't taking no for an answer.

The now wide-eyed women looked at Joelle, obviously

waiting to see if it was safe for them to leave. With her glare still fastened on Dallas, she nodded.

"We'll only be a minute," Joelle explained, making it sound like a threat. To him.

The woman holding the dress eased it onto a chair as if the darn thing might break in half, and she crept out with her friend. The moment the pair was out of the room, Dallas shut the door and locked it.

"I won't let you do this," Dallas began.

And Joelle knew what he meant. This had nothing to do with the wedding to a weasel. That was just an added irritation and even more of one because he shouldn't have cared a pig's hair if she was getting married.

But hell's Texas bells, she was marrying Owen.

Joelle threw off his grip and huffed. "You shouldn't have come."

"You didn't give me much of a choice. You didn't return my calls, and your hoity-toity sounding assistant said you were leaving on a monthlong honeymoon."

Her spicy brown eyes narrowed to the point that he was surprised she could even see him. "I didn't return your calls because there's nothing I can discuss with you."

"Wrong answer, try again," Dallas fired back. "We have plenty to discuss."

She opened her mouth, but her cell phone buzzed. She took a step toward the chair arm where the phone was lying, and Joelle looked at the caller ID on the screen. She mumbled some profanity. Dallas glanced at the screen, too, and he saw the call was from Owen.

"Excuse me a second," she grumbled, and snatched up the phone. "Everything's okay," she greeted her groom-to-be.

Dallas just listened. Except Joelle wasn't saying anything. Owen was doing all the talking, and Dallas couldn't make out a word the weasel was saying. But he could guess the gist of the one-sided conversation that was making every muscle in Joelle's body go stiff.

Owen likely wanted to know why Joelle's ex-lover was in her dressing room at the church just—Dallas checked the time—fifty-one minutes before she was to become Owen's bride.

"I'll take care of this," Joelle said, and she jabbed the end button. She whirled back around to face him. "You have to go."

As if that would get him to budge. "You're within days, maybe hours, of sending your report to the governor." Who also happened to be her boss.

A report that could crush Dallas a thousand times over.

She huffed again and put her hands on her hips. The move caused the sides of her robe to open in a vee, and he got a glimpse of a lacy white bra and her right nipple that the lace in no way concealed.

Dallas felt that old familiar tug, deep within his body, and he told that tug to take a fast hike. Joelle was no longer a woman he wanted in his bed.

And he was almost certain of that.

Almost.

But just in case he had doubts about it, he didn't have any doubts about the woman herself. Sexual stuff might still be lingering between them, but he didn't want her in his life.

No way.

She'd made her choice sixteen years ago. A choice that had broken his stupid teenage heart. And yeah, that was a long time ago, but forgiving and forgetting weren't what he saw himself doing when it came to Joelle. Actually, to anybody.

"The report?" he reminded her. Reminded himself,

too. And he cursed that blasted nipple-peek for distracting him.

"My report is just that, a *report* of my observations. The local sheriff at Rocky Creek is already investigating the case, but the governor wants to know if he should request the Texas Rangers to go in and assist. So he'll read what I've written and decide what to do."

No. It wasn't just a report. And as for the sheriff's investigation, that wasn't going anywhere. The sheriff had only been on the job a few months, had little experience in law enforcement. No. If anyone found anything incriminating, it'd be Joelle and her team of hotshot investigators that she had crawling all over the state.

Dallas aimed his index finger at her. "This report could destroy Kirby." His foster father. And a man he darn sure wouldn't see destroyed.

Joelle dodged his gaze, turned, and gave him another view of that blasted bra. The left nipple this time. Great day in the morning! He didn't need this.

Nor the other thing he saw.

He'd missed it at first because the pendant was literally tucked in her bra, but it shifted, slipped out, and he spotted the gold heart locket. Not a flashy piece, this one was coated with fine scratches and even a little tarnish. It looked like the one he'd given her for her sixteenth birthday, but he had to be wrong about that. And even if he wasn't, if it was indeed the same necklace, maybe it was the "something old" part of her bridal garb.

Dallas wondered whose picture was inside it now.

Definitely not his.

"This isn't a good time for the cat to get your tongue," Dallas reminded her.

Again, she opened her mouth to say something, but there was a knock at the door before she could get out even a syllable. Both of them groaned and cursed the interruption. At this rate, the day would be over before he got answers.

"Ignore it," Dallas insisted.

Another knock. "Joelle, it's me, Lindsey. Owen called and wanted me to check on you."

Joelle did the opposite of ignoring it. She stepped around him, unlocked the door and threw it open. The tall, curvy brunette peered in, first at Joelle and then at Dallas.

"Are you, uh, okay?" she asked Joelle.

"I'm fine," Joelle snapped. She followed the woman's gaze to the lacy bra, cursed again and jerked the robe shut. "My *friend* was just leaving."

"No. He's not," Dallas said. "Not until we get this straight."

Lindsey volleyed concerned looks between them, and she handed Joelle the plastic cup she was holding. "Jack Daniel's, straight up," she told Joelle. "I figured you could use it."

"I can." Joelle took the shot in one gulp. "I won't be long," she added, sounding even more riled than Dallas was.

Joelle whirled around, put her back to the door and faced him head-on. "I can't do this now. Please go."

The *please* gave him a few seconds pause. She hadn't said it in anger—something he knew firsthand that she was pretty good at—but rather in a breathy whisper. Still, he couldn't let a breathy plea stop him.

"We settle this now," he insisted.

She groaned and scratched her head, mussing more of that perfect hairdo. "If Kirby did something wrong all those years ago, then I can't keep it hidden away."

Something wrong? Yeah. More like something *right*.

"I'm sure I don't have to remind you, but sixteen years ago Kirby got me and my foster brothers out of that hellhole."

In this case, the hellhole was the Rocky Creek Children's Facility. A down-home name for a notorious orphanage that had nearly destroyed him.

"Kirby may have pulled strings to get custody of you," she added, then swallowed hard. "Not just you, but the others. Clayton, Harlan, Slade, Wyatt. And especially Declan."

All five of his foster brothers. Yeah, there might have been an irregularity or two in the paperwork that had given Kirby guardianship and then full custody. But if Kirby hadn't gotten them out, none of them might be alive right now. They sure as heck wouldn't all be deputy U.S. marshals and running a successful ranch.

"Kirby may have done some other things to make sure custody wasn't contested," Joelle added in a whisper.

Dallas knew exactly what she meant because he'd already gotten wind of her so-called report that the governor would use to determine if the Texas Rangers should open a full-scale investigation against Kirby. An investigation that could lead to some charges.

Including murder.

Now it was Dallas's turn to swallow hard. He couldn't let that happen to Kirby.

The photos of the dead man's bones flashed through his head. They'd been found seven weeks ago, a little over a mile from the now abandoned Rocky Creek facility. A crew working on the power lines had uncovered it.

Jonah Webb's body.

The devil of a man who'd once run Rocky Creek and someone who'd been missing for sixteen years.

"Jonah's rib cage showed signs of knife wounds," Joelle explained.

Something else he didn't need to be reminded of. And that brought back another set of images that Dallas would rather forget. "I read the forensic reports."

He'd also studied the police file and the official notification from the governor to authorize Joelle, one of the state's legal advisers, to conduct an independent inquiry to determine what had gone on at the state-run facility all those years ago.

"My father didn't kill Jonah Webb," Dallas concluded.

Something went through her eyes. Not a glare this time, but something he couldn't quite figure out. "The governor's a fair man."

That gave Dallas zero reassurance. "If there's something in your report that implicates my father, and I'm pretty sure there is, then the governor will have no choice but to make it an official investigation."

She blew out a long breath, swiped some of those now dangling strands of hair from her face.

He waited, mentally rehearsing the argument to make her amend that report. Or burn it. Or just plain lie. "Arresting my father wouldn't be justice, and you know it."

"Yes, but it would be the law," she snapped.

"To hell with the law." Dallas nearly winced at his own words. He was a federal marshal, sworn to obey the very laws that might take his father from him.

He forced himself to regain what little composure he could. "My father's not in good health and might not survive something like this." That caused the anger to roar through him again. "You can stop it now."

She shook her head, and yet something different went through her eyes. Not emotion exactly, but she got a weird glazed look.

Joelle touched her fingers to her forehead, and the plastic cup slipped from her hand and clattered onto the hardwood floor. "You have to go."

Like the *please,* that was all breath.

Dallas looked at the cup on the floor. At the dress. And then at her. "What's going on?"

"I'm marrying Owen," she said. Still whispered, except this time there was a tremble in her voice. Her hands were shaking, too.

Dallas caught her arm. "What's wrong?"

She shook her head, and her eyelids fluttered down. "I think someone drugged me." Her words were so slurred that it took him a moment to realize what she'd said.

"Drugged you?"

Ah, hell.

What the devil was going on here?

"It's not safe for either of us," she mouthed through those trembling peach-tinged lips.

And with that, Joelle crumpled right into his arms.

Chapter Two

Joelle couldn't stop herself from falling. The dizziness hit her hard and fast, and if Dallas hadn't caught her, she would have dropped to the floor.

Oh, mercy.

The drink had been drugged with something. She was sure of it. But she couldn't take the time to berate herself for downing it like water.

She had to get Dallas out of there *now*.

"You have to go," she repeated. Except she hardly recognized her own words. She sounded like a drunk. Felt like one, too.

"I'm not going anywhere," Dallas snarled, and he scooped her up in his arms.

Joelle shook her head and prayed she could convince him to leave. Unfortunately, her mouth was partly numb, and the words didn't come.

"Who drugged you?" he demanded. "Why did you say it wasn't safe for either of us?"

She'd said that last part because her suddenly fuzzy brain had let it slip. As for the first question, she knew who was responsible for this, but telling Dallas that would open a Pandora's box that should remain closed.

Joelle prayed that whatever drug she'd been given would wear off quickly and that it wouldn't be harmful.

Dallas carried her across the room, deposited her on the love seat and took out his cell phone. "I'm calling an ambulance."

"No!" Joelle used every bit of her strength, which wasn't much, to latch on to his wrist. "You can't. I'll be okay. Just give me a second to catch my breath."

He stared at her, those intense blue eyes drilling holes in her and with the familiar star badge on his belt right in her face. Both Dallas and the badge were swimming in and out of focus, but Joelle knew that neither was going anywhere until she gave him some kind of explanation.

Or rather until she gave him a lie.

It had to be a quick one since she figured Owen would be there in ten minutes or less.

"I've been having anxiety attacks," she said, and the lie began. "Lindsey probably saw one coming on and gave me my meds in the drink." To add some detail to the lie, she dropped her head back on the love seat arm. "I need a quick nap before the wedding."

But more than that, she needed Dallas gone.

He still didn't budge. Dallas stood there, all six feet three inches of him. A real Texas cowboy cop as his name implied, in his jeans, white button-down shirt and cowboy boots. Oh, and the midnight-black Stetson that was the same color as his rumpled hair.

Because she'd seen him stark naked, she knew that black hair was sprinkled on his chest. She also knew he had a body that could make her go all hot. His body hadn't been the issue when they'd been together as teenagers. Nor the sex. With Dallas, it'd been powder keg and fireworks.

The problem had been with, well, everything else.

Dallas glanced at her wedding dress again, the cup on the floor and then his lethal stare came back to her.

No.

Even through the whirlwind in her head, Joelle could see that he was piecing together things that should never be pieced.

"Why are you marrying Owen?" He used his marshal's voice, the one that had no doubt gotten him many confessions.

She'd have to lie again. Except this one would be a whopper. "Because I love him."

Joelle hoped she sounded believable, but judging from Dallas's worsening glare, she hadn't even come close.

"I'm pregnant," she tried again.

He stooped down, violating her personal space, and he put his face just inches from hers. "Liar. If you were pregnant, you wouldn't have had a shot of Jack Daniel's."

He had her on that particular lie, but Joelle still had to do something, *anything,* to convince him to leave. "Go, please, for old times' sake."

"You don't have any old times' sake favors left. You're the one who walked out on me, and now you're trying to destroy my father."

She started to shake her head, but it only made the dizziness worse so she stopped. It made the dizziness worse to sit up as well, but Joelle had to keep watching out the front window for Owen.

Dallas took out his phone again. "Tell me why you said it wasn't safe for either of us, or I'm calling that ambulance now."

Joelle pressed her fingertips to her temples to calm the storm inside. "Because Owen is jealous of you. And he has a bad temper." That was the truth, on both counts.

"Yeah. He does." And that's all Dallas said for several heart-stopping moments. "If you're so scared of him, then why are you marrying him? And don't give me that non-sense about loving him."

"But I do love him," she insisted. Of course, it was another Texas-size lie.

Dallas made a skeptical sound in his throat and went to press the buttons on his phone. Joelle couldn't let him make that call.

"Don't." She grabbed his arm and put some steel in her voice. Well, as much steel as she could manage considering the drug haze was taking over her entire body.

"When I look at you…" She had to pause and force her mouth to work. "Uh, I think of all those years it took me to get over you. I, um, feel the hurt…the anger."

"You feel all that, huh?" he growled.

"All that." Joelle hoped these words she was trying to say would make enough sense to get him to leave. "I feel disgusted with myself." Another pause. "Disgusted that you wouldn't give me a second chance."

"I don't give second chances. *Ever.*"

"Believe me, I know. You're not capable of forgiveness. You're a cold, hard man, Dallas Walker."

There. She'd gotten it all out. Yes, it stung to say that, but it was God's honest truth, and maybe the truth would hurt him enough to get those cowboy boots moving toward the door.

It didn't.

Mercy. Joelle had to take another verbal jab at him. She also had to take another breath before she continued. "I'll bury the report that I'm supposed to give to the governor. Kirby is safe. Now, get the heck out of here."

That should have done it. Should have gotten Dallas moving to leave. But he just kept staring at her.

Joelle cursed. The dizziness was getting worse, and she would probably lose consciousness soon.

"I hate you," she managed to say.

And she wished that were true. Except at the moment she did hate him for not doing something he had to do—*leave.*

"I will get to the bottom of this," Dallas threatened. He huffed, and his expression softened. "But I need to call that ambulance so you can go to the hospital. If Owen has a hissy fit because I'm here, then I'll protect you from him."

"You can't." But Joelle was instantly sorry she'd said that.

There it was again. That flash in his lawman's eyes. She was digging her own grave here.

And his.

Think.

She had to do something to defuse this situation.

If she could get into the adjoining bathroom, maybe she could crawl out the window and go to the front of the church where Owen would soon arrive. She could kiss him while Dallas watched. It would turn her stomach to do that, but it might be the very thing to convince Dallas to leave so that she could go through with the vows.

Joelle shoved her elbows against the love seat so she could lever herself up. Not easily. But she managed to get to her feet by holding on to the armrest. "I have to go to the bathroom."

He stared at her. "I'll go with you."

She huffed. "I have to *go* to the bathroom. I don't need company for that."

"No, but you do need help. You can't walk."

True. But that wouldn't stop her.

Well, hopefully not.

She let go of the armrest but immediately had to catch

onto something or she would have fallen. Unfortunately, she caught onto Dallas.

Joelle was suddenly engulfed in his strong arms. And against his chest. Her face landed right against his neck, and she drew in his scent with the breath that she fought to take. It was a scent she knew too well, one that triggered old thoughts and feelings that could never be triggered again.

"Sorry," she mumbled when her hand landed against the front of his jeans. She mumbled another apology when she realized her robe had fallen open and that his hand was now against the lacy side panel of her bra.

Judging from the way his breathing changed, Dallas was battling some old triggers, too. Normally, that would have pleased her; after all, he'd crushed her heart all those years ago. Tormenting him was something she'd fantasized about doing.

But there was nothing gratifying about this situation.

Besides, she'd crushed his heart, too.

Joelle pushed herself away from him and slapped her hand on the wall. She used it for support so she could make her way to the bathroom. Thankfully, the door was already ajar because just seconds before Dallas had arrived, Joelle had been using the mirror to touch up her hair and makeup. Something she would have to do again.

She still had to go through with those vows.

Each step was a major effort, but Joelle finally made it inside the tiny bathroom. She used her elbow to shut the door. Managed, somehow, to lock it. And then made as much of a beeline as possible toward the window.

The dizziness was getting worse, maybe because she was moving, but Joelle tried to fight her way through it. Then she tripped over the bunched up rug and landed with a thud against the windowsill.

"Joelle?" Dallas called out. He knocked on the door. "You okay?"

"Fine," she lied.

She anchored her body against the wall, lifted the window and pushed out the screen. It would be a tight fit, but there was no other option. She climbed onto the toilet seat to lever herself up.

"Joelle!" Dallas shouted again. "To hell with modesty. Open up so I can see you."

"In a second. I'm almost done."

Joelle got her arm through the window and looked down at the ground. Not a long drop, but she doubted she'd land on her feet. She got the other arm on the sill.

Just as there was a loud cracking sound behind her.

She looked over her shoulder to see that Dallas had kicked down the door. He had his gun drawn, and his gaze fired around the tiny room. He cursed and reholstered his gun when he saw that she was alone.

"Where the hell do you think you're going?" he demanded.

But he didn't wait for an answer. He hurried to her, hauled her onto his shoulder caveman style and carried her back into the dressing room.

That's when she saw the dark green Range Rover squeal to a stop in front of the church.

Owen.

Joelle struggled to get out of Dallas's grip, but he held on and turned to see what had captured her attention. Owen, dressed in a tux, stepped from the vehicle and walked toward the men who worked for him. She had only seconds now to diffuse this mess.

She watched as Owen spoke to his *employees*. The bald one pointed to the window, but she hoped Dallas and she were too far away for Owen to see them.

"I have to talk to him," she insisted.

"No. You don't," Dallas disagreed.

Joelle groaned because that was the pigheaded tone she'd encountered too many times to count.

"I'll be the one to talk to Owen," Dallas informed her. "I want to find out what's going on."

Joelle managed to slide out of his grip and put her feet on the floor. She latched on to his arm to stop him from going to the door. "You can't. You have no idea how bad things can get if you do that."

He stopped, and stared at her. "Does all of this have something to do with your report to the governor?"

She blinked, but Joelle tried to let that be her only reaction. "No."

More staring. Before Dallas glanced out the window. Owen had finished talking to his men and turned toward the church steps. She was down to mere seconds now. Not much time to get Dallas out of there.

"Are you going to tell me what this is all about?" Dallas demanded.

"I can't. It's too dangerous." Joelle was ready to start begging him to leave. But she didn't have time to speak.

Dallas hooked his arm around her, lifted her and tossed her back over his shoulder.

"What are you doing?" Joelle tried to get away, tried to get back on her feet, but he held on tight.

Dallas threw open the dressing room door and started down the hall with her. "I'm kidnapping you."

Chapter Three

There was a split second of time where Dallas thought about what he was doing. And what he was doing was a crime.

A felony, no less.

He didn't consider himself a lawbreaker, but he had stretched and bent it a few times to get justice. And for that split second he wondered if there was a different way to go about this. He didn't want to call his foster brothers and involve them, but he did consider calling the locals. He knew the sheriff was a fair man.

But this wasn't exactly a fair situation.

No. He couldn't involve the locals because there wasn't enough time to get them out to the church to stop this. Plus, Dallas had to stay with Joelle, to convince her not to release that report. If given the chance, Owen would just whisk her away, and Dallas figured Owen—and apparently Joelle, too—would do anything and everything to prevent him from seeing her in the near future. The report would be released, and Kirby would be arrested.

That was a solid enough reason to get her away from Owen, but then he heard Owen's footsteps in the church entry and listened to Joelle's slurred, drugged protests to let her go.

And Dallas had no choice.

It wasn't safe for her to be here. It wasn't safe for him to involve law enforcement. And that meant he had to get out of there fast.

Dallas didn't know what was going on, but he was pretty sure he wouldn't get the answers from Owen. He had a long, bad history with the man he'd once shared a room with at the orphanage, and that history wouldn't get better. In fact, it was about to come to a hot boil if he learned that Owen was the one who'd drugged Joelle.

Yeah.

He would *bend* the law to get back at Owen for doing that.

Dallas passed by the room where the two wedding attendants were hovering. They were no doubt aware that something bad was in the air, but they didn't run out to try to rescue Joelle.

Later, he'd want to know why.

For now, he had enough questions and very little time to get Joelle out of there so he could get some answers. Answers that didn't involve lies about loving Owen and a feigned pregnancy.

"Where you takin' me?" Joelle asked. The slurring was getting worse, and when she hit her fists against his back, they landed like limp thuds.

Dallas made his way through the back corridors that had been built as additions to the old Victorian church. He knew the way because he'd used the halls to find his foster brother, Declan, when he'd sneak out for a smoke when he was supposed to be attending Sunday school.

"Owen," Joelle mumbled.

And for a moment Dallas thought she'd seen her groom. A glance over his shoulder verified they had the hall to themselves. But he did hear Owen calling out for her. It wouldn't be long before Owen made his way to them.

Dallas bolted out the back door and past the catering truck that was carting stuff into the fellowship hall. No doubt where the reception was supposed to be held. It was a cheap and plain venue for a man as stinkin' rich as Owen.

But there were a lot of fishy things about this wedding.

Two guys carrying a wedding cake looked over at Dallas, but he only pointed to his badge. He didn't speak to them, didn't slow down. Dallas ran across the groomed back lawn where, over the years, he'd attended church picnics and chatted up a few girls.

There was a heavily treed area just ahead, and Dallas raced into it. Not in a straight line. That's because he figured Owen or one of his armed goons had already made it to the back of the church, and Dallas didn't want them to be able to pinpoint his position.

Or guess where he was going.

After all, Owen knew these woods, too, since he'd lived in Maverick Springs for more than a dozen years.

"Dallas, this is wrong," Joelle mumbled.

Yeah, it was, but it would be equally wrong to leave her there without the answers to his questions. Maybe when he had those answers, he could figure out a way to stop her from pressing charges against him.

Dream on.

Once the effects of the drug wore off, she'd be one riled woman.

Even over Joelle's mumbles, Dallas heard Owen's shouts and the rushing water of Butcher Creek just ahead. He didn't go in that direction. Owen would expect it. Instead, Dallas headed west where the woods were thick, and the fallen leaves and lack of sun would make it harder for them to be tracked.

Joelle quit squirming, quit mumbling, and this time Dallas did stop so he could make sure she was still breathing. She was, thank goodness. But she was pale and practically unconscious.

Hell.

He needed to get her to the doctor.

But it wouldn't be easy. He had to cut through the woods and head to the old cabin that Declan kept when he needed to get away. There was a four-wheeler parked there. It wouldn't be ideal transportation for an unconscious woman in a bathrobe, but it would have to do. Plus, it would probably turn out to be faster than going back to Owen for help.

Dallas didn't think Owen would be in a helping mood.

The temperature dropped when they reached the thick part of the woods where there was no sunlight at all. So he wrapped his arms around Joelle's legs. Maybe that and his body heat would keep her warm.

"Are you taking me to bed?" she mumbled.

Even groggy, she'd asked a question that brought back those blasted bad memories. Or good ones, depending on his mood. Right now, his mood sucked, and he didn't want to think of the times he had indeed hauled her off to bed.

But he did.

He thought about it.

And cursed himself.

"Dallas?" he heard Owen call out.

Owen yelled something else that Dallas couldn't make out. Something bad, no doubt. Joelle had been right about her fiancé having a vile temper. When they'd lived at the orphanage, Dallas had not only witnessed it, he'd been on the receiving end of it—often while trying to run interference for the younger boys who would later become his foster brothers.

He thought of his brothers as he ran. Also thought of his father. Kirby wasn't going to approve of this, but his brothers would stand with him. They would understand, and if they'd had the chance to save Kirby, any one of them would do the exact same thing.

Dallas kept running, the minutes ticking off in his head, still not taking a direct route to the cabin. He meandered through the woods, trying to leave as few signs as possible so that Owen and his henchmen couldn't easily track them.

He finally spotted the cabin just ahead. Good thing, too, because his legs were about to give out. He checked the shed first and saw the four-wheeler parked inside before he carried Joelle onto the porch. He located the key that Declan kept in a goofy frog planter, and he let himself in.

"Where are we?" Joelle mumbled.

"The place belongs to Declan."

The cabin wasn't much, just one room and a bath with sparse furnishings. He eased Joelle onto the sofa sleeper and went in search of a jacket for her and the keys to the four-wheeler.

When Dallas turned around, Joelle was sitting up. Or, rather, she was trying to. She was wobbly, but she finally got herself upright.

She stared at him, dragged her tongue over her bottom lip and added a groan. "You really screwed up this time."

Dallas grabbed a ratty-looking jacket from a hook on the wall. "Well, I'm not alone. Your fiancé just had you drugged, and you're scared to death of him."

She didn't deny either of those things.

And that meant he had more questions for the nonanswers she'd just given.

Joelle shivered, pulled her knees up to her chest and hugged herself.

Oh, man.

There it was. That punch of sympathy. As long as Joelle was defiant and lying through her teeth, he could hold on to the anger over that blasted report of her inquiry. But seeing her weak and trembling wasn't good for his resolve of wanting to wring her neck.

Dallas huffed, took the jacket to her and draped it over her shoulders. Even though they needed to get out of there, he sat down beside her. "Why did Owen drug you?"

She opened her mouth. Closed it. Then, shook her head. "Long story."

"We have time," he lied.

Her gaze came to his, and he saw the tears. Yep, tears. He would have had to be a heartless SOB to be immune to those. Dallas cursed, slipped his arm around her, and Joelle went to him as if she belonged there.

She didn't, he reminded himself. The ring on her finger and the report she'd written were proof of that.

"I need to marry Owen," Joelle whispered. She moved away from him. "I don't have a choice. And neither do you."

Dallas frowned. "What the heck does that mean?"

"It means you have to take me back to the church, and then you have to leave."

Well, there went that shot of empathy he'd had just seconds earlier. "Have you lost your mind? The man drugged you," he reminded her in case she'd missed it the first time he'd said it. "There's no good reason for you to become his wife."

Her gaze came to his again. "Yes, there is. And don't ask the reason because you don't want to know."

That caused him to shake his head. "You're wrong about that. In fact, we're not leaving this place until you tell me what's going on."

"I can't." She didn't even hesitate.

Dallas stood and went to look for the key to the four-wheeler. It was a better use of his time than sitting there glaring at her stubborn face and listening to her ramblings that didn't make sense. But getting up didn't stop the thought from coming at him.

No pregnancy, so why would a woman marry a man she didn't love? A jerk who would drug her? There was only one reason that popped into his head.

Because that man had forced her into it.

But why would Owen have done that? Again, he could only think of one reason: Owen wanted something from her.

Joelle wasn't rich, but she had a job with power and access to the governor. Owen was wealthy, always wheeling and dealing, so perhaps he needed Joelle to cut some corners for him. Maybe along the lines of tax exemptions or reclassification of land that he planned to buy for commercial purposes.

So, yeah, there were reasons why Owen would want Joelle in his bed and under his influence.

But why would Joelle have agreed?

The answer came quickly, too.

Because Owen was blackmailing her or using some other form of coercion.

Dallas rifled through the kitchen cabinets and located the key for the four-wheeler inside the sole coffee cup. They could go now. He could take Joelle to the hospital and face whatever consequences would come from the fallout. On the way there, he could talk her out of submitting a report that would lead to his father's arrest.

That was a must.

He couldn't let her go until he was positive that Kirby wouldn't be hauled off to jail.

"The report," Dallas repeated under his breath. And he turned back around to face her. "Are you marrying Owen because of that report?"

She dodged his gaze, and he knew he'd hit pay dirt.

Dallas walked closer. "You dug into the old orphanage records when you were researching that report. You no doubt found out that right before Webb disappeared, Kirby was about to launch an investigation into the abuse going on there."

And there was one other thing she would have done.

"You also dug through the documents connected to Kirby's filing for guardianship of me and my foster brothers," Dallas added.

He stooped down again, cupped her chin and forced her to make eye contact. Her pupils were still dilated, but he had no doubt that she had understood every single word he'd said.

"Kirby probably cut some corners when he did that guardianship paperwork," Dallas admitted. "He did that to save us. Heck, he saved you, too, and got you into a good foster home." He paused. "Are you marrying Owen because of something you found during your inquiry?"

Joelle didn't answer. She tried to look away, but Dallas held her chin so she couldn't move. Still, she squeezed her eyes shut.

Dallas had to press harder. "Are you marrying Owen to save Kirby?"

Joelle opened her eyes, her gaze nailed to his. "No." A shivery sound left her mouth. "I'm marrying Owen to save *you*."

Chapter Four

Joelle heard the words come out of her mouth, but she couldn't believe she'd actually said them aloud.

To Dallas, no less.

She'd spoken the truth—for one of the first times today—but it was a truth that Dallas shouldn't have heard. It wouldn't make things easier. Just the opposite. Because now Dallas would demand an explanation.

Something she couldn't give him.

Joelle closed her eyes and tried to think. It was next to impossible. Everything inside her was spinning, and she doubted she could stand up, much less try to run.

"What was in that drink?" she asked.

"I think you know," Dallas answered. "Someone drugged you. Owen, no doubt."

Yes, and for her there wasn't a shred of doubt. Owen had done this, or rather he'd gotten Lindsey to do it for him. That infuriated her. Joelle had known she couldn't trust Lindsey. For Pete's sake, the woman worked for Owen and was probably in love with him. But she hadn't thought for one second that Lindsey would resort to something like this.

"How the heck could your marrying Owen save *me?*" Dallas demanded.

Joelle heard him moving around, and when she opened

her eyes again, Dallas was right in front of her face. So close that she could see the flecks of gray in his mostly blue eyes. She could see the determination there, too, and knew a lie wasn't going to fix this.

The truth wouldn't, either.

If fact, the truth would make this situation explode like an oil rig fire, and finding a way to dodge that fire was going to be tough.

Dallas stared at her. Cursed. And moved back. "I need to get you to the hospital."

That would only make things worse because it would get the sheriff involved. Joelle grabbed his wrist, and even though she didn't have much strength in her wobbly grip, she pulled him back down so that he was kneeling on the floor beside her. Not exactly a brilliant move. They were touching now, and that was never a good idea when it came to Dallas and her.

Even in its drugged state, her body thought it might get lucky. It wouldn't. And she was reasonably sure Dallas would agree.

"I don't need to go to the hospital." She hoped that was true, anyway. "Owen wouldn't have given me a drug that could kill me. My guess is whatever was in that drink, it was meant to daze me so I wouldn't be able to hear any argument you have to putting a stop to the wedding."

Dallas stared at her from beneath the brim of his Stetson. Except it wasn't just a stare. He seemed to be examining her. Maybe to make sure she wasn't about to succumb to the drug.

"Clearly, Owen isn't convinced of your love for him or he wouldn't have thought I stood a chance of talking you out of saying 'I do.'"

"Clearly," she repeated in a mumble. "But you didn't

talk. You took me hostage, and that means the damage control I have to do is…massive," Joelle settled for saying.

But the real word was *impossible*.

Still, she'd have to try because there wasn't an acceptable alternative. As soon as she gathered her wits enough to confront Owen, she'd try to resume their deal or work out a new one. For now though, Dallas was one confrontation too many.

"I need some water," she said. "And a few minutes to gather my breath. If I'm not feeling better soon, then I'll go to the hospital."

Dallas scowled as if he might refuse her on both counts, but it wasn't a delay tactic. Her throat was parched, and apparently she had some explaining to do. Plus, if she didn't start feeling better, she would indeed go to a hospital. But not the one in Maverick Springs and she wouldn't use her real name if she got treatment. She couldn't have this get back to Owen because he would retaliate in the worst possible way.

Cursing, Dallas went to the sink, got her the water, but as soon as he handed it to her, he went to the window and looked outside. Good move and something Joelle wished she'd thought of doing. Owen would indeed send someone to look for them.

"What are the chances Owen will find this cabin?" she asked, sipping the water.

"Extremely high." Dallas shot her a glance over his shoulder. "That means you give me that explanation you owe me, and then I get you out of here. First to the hospital and then so you can file charges against Owen for drugging you."

That got Joelle's complete attention. Well, as much as her drugged mind would allow. "I can't file charges against Owen."

"Then I will."

And Dallas would do exactly that if Joelle didn't talk, and talk fast. But where to start? This was a tangled mess, and she wasn't exactly at her best now when it came to winning an argument with Dallas.

"Remember when you were seventeen and Jonah Webb gave you a beating for sassing him?" she asked.

Dallas eased back around to face her, and his eyes were slightly narrowed. Probably because it wasn't a good memory to bring up. But that incident, that specific memory, was where the tangle really started to get bad.

"I didn't *sass* him," Dallas growled. "Webb beat up Declan for sassing him, and I told Webb if he laid another hand on Declan that I'd kill him. Webb punched me, and I punched him back until his goons held me down and let Webb have a go at me."

Yes, he had. And at the time Joelle had supported Dallas one hundred percent. Declan had only been thirteen and scrawny at that. Webb had been a hulk of a man. A brute and a grown-up bully who had no right or reason to assault any of the kids at Rocky Creek.

But Webb had done just that.

And often.

That day, he'd had Dallas beaten within an inch of his life. A strong motive for murder. It didn't look good, either, that Webb had gone missing that very night.

"Owen witnessed the threat you made to Webb," Joelle continued. "And he insisted I include it in my report to the governor."

"Of course he did." Dallas added more profanity. "Owen's a snotty-nosed tattletale. But hell's bells, tell me you aren't marrying Owen because of that?"

"No." Joelle needed another sip of water before she could continue. "When I started the report, I requested background checks on all persons of interest. Including Owen. One of his disgruntled business associates tipped off my investigator that Owen might not be the upstanding citizen he claimed to be. I personally did some digging and uncovered a few things, including some shady land and business deals."

Dallas didn't give her the surprised look she'd expected. "Yeah. Owen's dirty," he agreed. "I'd bet my favorite mare on that. And he's used the money that he inherited from his late wife and in-laws to do plenty of things I wish I could arrest him for. If you've got anything of a federal nature that I can use, I want it."

"I can't give it to you."

That earned her a flat look. "We're going to the hospital. Obviously, the drug has affected you pretty bad if you're covering for Owen."

"I'm not covering for him."

The flat look got flatter. "If it quacks like a duck, it's a duck."

And with that smart-mouthed reply, Dallas came across the room, set her water aside and lifted her to her feet. The dizziness returned with a vengeance, and Joelle had no choice but to lean on him. This time she took in his scent. And the feel of the muscles in his arms and chest.

Heck, she took him in, too, because all the memories came flooding back. Not of the fight with Webb or the miserable times they'd had at Rocky Creek but other times, when she'd been in his arms for a completely different reason.

He made a sound, a sort of grunt, and she hoped that didn't mean he was remembering things best forgotten.

Like the last night they'd had together at the creek.

No.

Best not to think of that.

"The hospital," Dallas growled. He yanked out his phone, no doubt to call either the hospital or one of his brothers, but he looked at the screen and grumbled something about not having service. It made sense because the cabin wasn't exactly on the beaten path.

He shoved his phone back in his pocket. "After I drop you off at the hospital, I can arrest Owen for trying to intimidate you into withholding evidence. Last time I checked that's called obstruction of justice."

"It's the same as what you want me to do for Kirby by killing that report," she reminded him.

"Yeah," he readily admitted.

Dallas didn't have to say more. He would put himself in the line of legal fire for Kirby—real fire, too—for the man who'd saved him from Rocky Creek. And that's why Joelle dug in her heels when they made it to the door. She'd fought too hard for Dallas to throw himself under a bus that he didn't even know was headed his way.

"There's more," she said, still leaning against him. Still taking in his scent. But she eased the memories onto the back burner. Way back. Because she couldn't have that playing into what else she had to tell him.

Dallas didn't roll his eyes, but he came close. "There's nothing you can say that'll stop me from going after Owen."

"Yes, there is."

That halted him for just a moment, but then he huffed and opened the door. He glanced around, those lawman's eyes checking for any sign of Owen or his men. Joelle tried to check, too, but her main focus was getting Dallas through what she was about to tell him.

It would change everything.

"Owen has a knife locked away in a safe-deposit box," she said. Dallas made a mild sound of interest and scooped her up, taking her toward the shed. "He said he got it from Webb's office the night he disappeared," she continued. "That it was lying on the floor and he took it."

"Good, now I can add petty theft to the charges I'll file against Owen," Dallas mumbled. He opened the shed and climbed onto the four-wheeler with her, positioning her in his lap.

"The knife has Webb's blood on it," Joelle added. "And fingerprints. *Yours.*"

That stopped him from starting the engine. Even though everything was still swimming in and out of focus, Joelle tried to catalog every bit of his reaction. He blinked, drew in his breath and then shook his head.

"Owen's lying," Dallas concluded.

Joelle had had the same reaction when Owen had first dropped the bombshell on her. "He's not. Not about this, anyway. I had the knife tested. It's your prints, all right. Webb's blood, too. His DNA was in the database because his wife had provided a hair sample to the cops when he went missing."

With her arm and shoulder against his chest, she could feel his heart thudding. Hers was, too. But she could also see the wheels turning in his head, and Dallas no doubt knew what conclusions she'd reached.

She hadn't wanted to go there, but the evidence was pretty damning.

"I had a friend run the tests," she explained. "It's all under wraps, and it'll stay secret—"

"Owen somehow faked the prints," Dallas interrupted. "Maybe the blood, too."

Joelle shook her head. "My friend was thorough, and the prints were badly smeared, but they have the pressure impressions consistent with the knife being in your hand."

She had to pause again. "And the blood, well, it's consistent with the blade being plunged into Webb's body."

She didn't have to remind him that there had indeed been knife marks found on Webb's ribs.

Dallas cursed. "You think I killed Webb."

Joelle hated that she even had to ask the question. "Did you?" But she didn't wait for an answer, and she wasn't sure she wanted to hear it anyway. "Webb was a horrible excuse for a human being. He deserved to die, and if he'd lived, he would have eventually killed you or one of the others."

Dallas grabbed her by the shoulders and hauled her up so they were facing each other. "I did not murder Webb."

Everything inside her went still, and she stared at Dallas, trying to figure out if that was true.

"I have no reason to lie to you," he added.

He did indeed have a reason because she would be duty bound to report his confession to the authorities. But she saw nothing in his eyes, his expression or his body language to indicate he'd killed Jonah Webb.

"Oh, God," she mumbled.

"Yeah. Let me guess—Owen said if you married him that he'd keep the knife hidden away, that I wouldn't be arrested for murder."

She managed a nod.

But Dallas only managed a stare. He looked at her as if the moon had just come crashing down on her head. "Why the hell would you have done that for me?" he asked. But as she'd done, he didn't give her a chance to answer. "You left me sixteen years ago without so much as a word as to where you were going or why I was no longer good enough for you."

"It wasn't like that," she blurted out.

He waited, obviously hoping she'd explain further, but

Joelle just shook her head. This was not the time to rehash the past, but she owed him something. "I just wanted you to have a fresh start."

That didn't ease the anger in his eyes. "And that couldn't have happened if you'd stayed?"

"No." And Joelle had no doubts about that. "You always talked about making something of yourself. About how important that was—"

"I could have made something of myself without you breaking things off."

"Not true," she argued. "You would have given me the time and energy you needed to devote to getting your life together. You'd been at Rocky Creek for nearly five years, you were about to turn eighteen and you'd just gotten a scholarship to college. I had another year of high school that I'd spend with a foster family over a hundred miles from where you'd be. I didn't want to hold you back."

"Admirable," he said, his tone stinging with bitterness.

"Not really. It was a fresh start for me, too." She met his gaze when she said that. "And I did come back, to try to mend fences with you."

A horrible idea. She'd visited him the summer of her freshman year of college. Why, she didn't know. *Wait.* She did know. She had missed him and wanted to say how sorry she was for the way things had turned out. Joelle had planned on using the young and stupid defense.

"It was too late to mend anything. I'd moved on by then," he grumbled.

"Yes, her name was Sandy if I remember correctly." And she hated that pang of jealousy even now. Hated that she was reliving things best left in the past. "You started this conversation, but is this really something you want to discuss?" Joelle challenged.

His jaw muscles stirred. His mouth tightened, and Dallas finally shook his head.

Good.

Because Joelle wanted it dropped now. It was hard to defend the decisions she'd made when she was seventeen.

"Even if Owen somehow managed to fake the evidence on that knife," she said, getting them back to what they should be discussing, "he would use it against you. Against me, too."

"You?" he snapped.

"Because I concealed the lab report. I didn't intend to conceal it permanently," she added quickly. "Just long enough so I could figure out who really did kill Webb."

"And who did?" Dallas pressed.

She had to shake her head. "I honestly don't know. But I worked out a deal with Owen," Joelle explained. "If I marry him, I can't be forced to testify against him regarding anything I learned during my investigation. And he won't testify against me for delaying the release of any evidence I found."

Dallas looked down at her. He didn't have to voice his displeasure. She could feel it in every solid inch of him. He started cursing again, and he jabbed the keys into the ignition of the four-wheeler and started it.

"You were a fool to trust Owen," she heard him say even over the roar of the engine.

They barreled out of the shed and onto the trail that she figured would take them back to town. Dallas was obviously still determined to get her to the hospital.

And then arrest Owen.

Then Owen would have Dallas arrested.

That would mean she would be exactly where she'd fought so hard not to be—with Dallas in jail and Owen pretty much calling the shots about the release of the knife and evidence.

"The knife looked familiar," she said, but she wasn't sure he heard her. Later, she'd have to make him hear.

She'd also have to put a stop to his plans to arrest Owen.

Somehow.

And maybe she could do that merely by describing the knife, by telling Dallas her suspicions about whose it was. Except it was much more than a suspicion.

Joelle was fairly certain, and if she was right, then all the evidence would only lead to multiple arrests.

"You have to stop this," she begged Dallas.

He went board stiff, and for a moment Joelle thought she'd gotten through his thick skull. He threaded the four-wheeler into a cluster of trees on the banks of a stream, then stopped and killed the engine. When she opened her mouth to ask why he'd done.that, he touched his fingers to his lips in a stay-quiet gesture. He also shoved her behind him on the seat and drew his gun.

Alarmed at both the gestures and the concerned look in his eyes, Joelle followed his gaze back to the cabin.

And that's when she saw the two men.

They were dressed in dark clothes, and both were carrying rifles. It definitely wasn't Owen or the armed *assistants* he'd had with him back at the church, but Joelle had no doubts that they worked for Owen. They'd come looking for Dallas and for her.

One of the men looked directly at them, and she sucked in her breath, waiting for them to demand that Dallas drop his gun so they could take her back to Owen. Instead, the man said something to his comrade.

And then they both trained those rifles on Dallas and her.

Chapter Five

Hell. This was not how Dallas wanted this to go down.

Joelle was still half-dazed, and they were miles from town with no phone service for him to call for backup and help. Now he had to deal with two armed bozos who no doubt worked for the very man Dallas wanted to arrest.

After what Joelle had just told him about Owen blackmailing her, it wasn't a surprise that her *fiancé* had wanted to stop her from talking.

Or stop her from backing of the marriage.

But Dallas was a little surprised that Owen would order his men to aim rifles at a federal marshal, especially when that marshal knew exactly what a dirt wad Owen really was.

In hindsight, he should have already gotten Joelle out of the woods and back to town, but Dallas had been so anxious to hear her explanation as to why she was marrying a weasel that he'd now let that weasel get the drop on them.

Later, he'd kick himself for that Texas-size mistake. But for now, he had a situation to contain.

"Put down your gun," one of the bozos warned. He was lean and mean-looking like his partner, but they weren't the men who'd been back at the church. "And drop those keys for the four-wheeler."

If he'd been alone, Dallas wouldn't have considered giving up without a fight, but he didn't want Joelle in the middle of a shootout.

"You do know who I am, right?" Dallas pointed toward his badge just in case their boss hadn't filled them in on who they were dealing with.

"You're a rogue marshal," the man answered. He took a step closer. "And you're to hand Ms. Tate over to us."

Dallas couldn't argue with the rogue part, but he sure as heck could with the rest. "Not a chance. She's in my protective custody."

Well, almost.

After everything she'd told him, Joelle certainly needed some kind of protection from Owen. Of course, Dallas had his own issues to work out with Owen and that blasted knife.

"I'll go with them," Joelle mumbled. "I don't want any trouble."

"Too late, trouble's here," Dallas told her. "And you're not going anywhere with them."

"Remember, Owen can have you arrested," she tried.

"Not if I arrest him first." That was the plan, anyway, but Dallas had to accept that he, too, could be taken into custody until all of this got sorted out. Still, it was a small price to pay to make sure Joelle didn't do something as stupid as marry Owen.

To protect Dallas, no less.

Well, to protect her, too, since Owen had threatened to have her arrested. But that was yet something else that wouldn't be worked out if he surrendered to these goons and let them haul Joelle back to Owen. He'd just force a hasty "I do" and then whisk her off somewhere so that Dallas couldn't get to her.

"Put down your gun," the man repeated.

"Or what?" Dallas answered. "You plan to shoot a lawman, huh?"

The two glanced at each other as if they might consider doing just that. And maybe they would. Obviously, Owen had been willing to go pretty darn far to get what he wanted and hide his criminal activity. Just in case Owen had given these two orders to shoot, Dallas kept his gun aimed at the guy who'd been doing the talking.

There was a snapping sound behind him, and while trying to keep an eye on the men in front of them, Dallas gave a quick glance over his shoulder. He'd hoped the sound had come from Joelle, but no such luck. It was the sound of footsteps, but he didn't even have time to fully turn toward them before he heard a gun go off.

Dallas cursed, hooked his left arm around Joelle and dragged her off the four-wheeler and to the ground. He came up ready to fire, but judging from the sound and angle of the shot, neither of them had fired it.

It'd come from behind Joelle and him.

And another shot quickly followed.

Dallas scrambled over Joelle, shoving her beneath him to protect her.

"They want me," she insisted. Obviously still under the stupid assumption that Dallas was going to let her surrender, she tried to get up. He pushed her right back down.

"Stay put," he warned her.

"But they're trying to kill us."

Except they weren't. Both bullets slammed into the tires of the four-wheeler, making the vehicle impossible to drive. And that was bad news because Dallas had planned on using it to make their escape.

"Drop your gun," the guy with the rifle repeated, "and no one will get hurt."

"You sure about that?" Dallas countered. "Because those bullets came darn close to hitting us."

The man made a sound of disagreement. "If he'd wanted you dead, you already would be."

And Dallas figured that was the sad truth.

He glanced all around, trying to pinpoint the shooter, but Dallas couldn't see anyone in the thick woods. Thanks to the spring growth, everything was in full leaf and bushy. Plenty of places for a shooter to hide. At least the shots hadn't come from the stream that was several yards below the embankment because if Joelle and he had to hoof it out of there, that stream was their best bet.

It was *negotiation* time.

"We're all going into Maverick Springs to talk this out," Dallas said, making sure it didn't sound like a suggestion but the order of an ornery lawman. Which he was, at this point. "Of course, all three of you, or however many the hell there are of you, are all under arrest. Your boss, too."

And he waited.

Joelle didn't say a word. Didn't move. However, Dallas could hear her breath gusting and feel her heart racing.

"No deal," one of the bozos in front of him finally answered. "Our orders are to deliver you back to the church. Both of you."

Now that was an interesting order, especially since someone at the church had probably noticed a ruckus going on and called the local cops. Dallas doubted that Owen could manage to silence everyone. Did Owen really think he could go through with those vows to a drugged bride and stand a snowball's chance of calling it a legal union?

Maybe.

And the problem was that Owen was pretty much in

control at the church. He had those three armed guards. Maybe more. It was the last place Dallas wanted to take Joelle since Owen could somehow neutralize him. Dallas didn't plan to be *neutralized* easily, but six gunmen were more than he wanted to face down with Joelle in tow.

"Get ready to move," Dallas whispered to her.

This would seriously test the gunman's assurance that no one was going to get hurt, but Dallas figured it was best to get Joelle out of there rather than risk what Owen had planned for her.

Joelle mumbled a "what?" but Dallas didn't answer her. They had to do this as fast as possible.

Using his body, he gave her a hard nudge, and together they rolled off the embankment and into the stream below. There wasn't much water—both a blessing and a curse. At least they wouldn't drown, but if the water had been deep with a strong current, it could have maybe whisked them away.

They landed hard, but Dallas tried to take the brunt of the fall. He didn't take even a second to breathe. He hooked his arm around Joelle's waist and got her sloshing through the ankle-deep water. Dallas went in the opposite direction of where he figured the shooter was still hiding.

"Hurry," he urged Joelle because he knew they didn't have much time before the gunmen made it to the embankment. Seconds at best.

And he needed to find some sort of cover so they could get some breathing room. He spotted a possible solution just ahead where the banks of the stream weren't so high. There was a pile of rocks, and the once-high water had shoved dead trees and limbs against them. It was wide enough to stop bullets. The thought had no sooner crossed his mind when he heard something else he didn't want to hear.

Another shot.

He shoved Joelle ahead of him in case the bullet came their way, but it didn't seem to land anywhere near them. Dallas didn't wait around to see if the shooter would get better aim; he latched on to Joelle and shoved her behind the rocks.

"I can talk to them," she said in between sucking in huge gulps of air.

"No, you can't."

But Joelle probably didn't hear him because more bullets came, and these smacked into the rocks. Man, they were loud, and that deafening noise didn't do much to steady Joelle's nerves. She was shaking now and mumbling a prayer.

Good.

They might need a little divine intervention before this was over.

"Marshal, you're making a mistake," someone called out when the shots finally stopped. Dallas recognized the voice. It was the same dirtbag who'd issued the other warnings. "Just put down your gun so we can end this."

Dallas ignored him and made a quick check of his phone. Still no service, which meant they were on their own in getting out of this. He looked around. Spotted their next move. A patch of trees with some dense underbrush. It was just ten yards away and in the direction he wanted to go because there was a main road less than a quarter of a mile away.

"We're heading there." Dallas tipped his head to the clump of oaks and hackberries.

Joelle nodded, but it was a wobbly one, and she was still shaking. Even though her eyes were no longer as glazed as they had been, he still wanted to get her to the hospital. Then he could make sure she was okay and have a blood test done to determine exactly what Owen had used to drug her.

Dallas didn't wait for another hail of bullets. He got Joelle moving toward the trees. No shots, but he did hear at least one of the gunmen cursing.

"This is a dangerous game you're playing, Marshal," the man shouted.

Dallas wanted to tell him that he wasn't the one playing here, but he didn't want to waste his breath. Plus, the gunmen could use the sound of his voice to pinpoint their exact location in the bushes. Unlike the rocks, the underbrush wouldn't give them much protection, and it was best not to do anything to get those bullets flying again.

He pointed to the next clump of trees and tipped his head to let Joelle know they were heading there next. Heck, if he had to, they'd just keep running and ducking behind the trees until they were all the way to the road.

"Joelle?" the man called out.

Great. Now the bozo was trying to bargain with a drugged woman. "Ignore him," Dallas told her.

She did. Joelle moved when he moved, and they darted behind the next set of trees.

"Joelle?" the guy repeated. "I know you can hear me. So can the marshal. And I don't think you're going to want him to hear what I'm about to say."

"Yeah, yeah," Dallas grumbled under his breath, and he got ready for their next round of evade and escape.

"I'm supposed to give you a message, Joelle," the man continued, his voice practically echoing through the woods. "Come back to the church with us now, or I'm to tell the marshal your dirty little secret."

Damn, the guy wasn't giving up.

Dallas immediately dismissed what the man said. But

Joelle didn't. She sucked in her breath hard, and her eyes widened. She shook her head.

And Dallas's stomach knotted.

Obviously, there was something to the dirty little secret threat. Part of him really wanted to know what had caused the color to drain from Joelle's already too-pale face. But the other part of him didn't want the guy to be able to use whatever he was trying to use to get her to cooperate.

"Let's go," Dallas insisted.

Joelle didn't argue. She practically leaped up from the ground, and even though she was still shaky, she ran as if her life depended on it. She didn't stop at the tree cluster, either. She kept moving and used the trees to help her stay on her feet.

"Running won't help," the man yelled. "One way or another, the marshal will find out what you did."

Joelle looked over at him, the tears shimmering in her eyes. "Don't ask, *please*," she said when Dallas opened his mouth.

Oh, hell.

This couldn't be good, but it was the worst possible time to push for information.

"The marshal will find out your secret," the man shouted. It was harder to hear his voice now, but Dallas seemed to have no trouble making out every word. "And if you think he'll protect you after he finds out what you did, you're wrong, Joelle. *Dead wrong.*"

Chapter Six

Everything inside Joelle was swirling, and she couldn't blame it entirely on the drugged drink. Those three words, *dirty little secret,* were repeating in her head just like the spray of bullets that the gunmen had fired into the rocks.

Mercy.

How had Owen learned *that?*

And better yet, how could she keep Dallas from asking her about it?

If he figured out the truth, it certainly wouldn't help matters. No way. Joelle needed to hurry to town so she could talk to Owen and try to defuse this situation before it blew up in all their faces.

"Keep moving," Dallas reminded her, and he shoved aside some low hanging tree limbs while he made another check over his shoulder.

Joelle checked, too, but she couldn't see the gunmen. That was something at least, but she knew that any second the bullets could start flying again.

They ran for what seemed like an eternity, and the woods and underbrush got even thicker. The bushes scraped at her robe and skin, reminders that she wasn't dressed for a trek through the wild. Of course, she hadn't planned on spending her day like this since she should have been standing in front of the altar by now.

So much for that plan.

Even over the roaring in her ears, Joelle heard something. Dallas apparently did, too, because he stopped so abruptly that she plowed right into him. He eased back more branches, and she saw the road.

And the truck.

The fear slammed through her again because she thought it could be one of Owen's men, but Dallas stepped out onto the road and flagged down the driver. When the truck braked to a stop, Joelle saw the familiar face behind the wheel.

Marshal Clayton Caldwell.

She'd not only known him for years since their time together at the Rocky Creek Children's Facility, he was also Dallas's foster brother.

"I've been out looking for you," Clayton said, his eyes widening a little when his gaze landed on her. "Didn't figure on seeing you, Joelle."

Not exactly a warm greeting, but then she hadn't expected warmth from any of Kirby's *boys*. Still, a frosty welcome was much better than facing the gunmen. But it didn't mean she was safe.

None of them were.

Dallas practically pushed her into the cab of the truck and moved her over so he could follow on the passenger's side. He kept watch of the surrounding woods. Kept his gun ready, too.

"There are three armed men probably following us," Dallas told his brother as Clayton made a quick call to let someone know that he'd found them. As soon as he finished, they sped away. "I need them brought in for questioning."

"Declan, Slade and Wyatt are all out looking," Clayton explained. "Can't contact them because they're in dead zones, but if the men are still out there, they'll find them. These guys took shots at you?"

"Oh, yeah," Dallas confirmed. "But I'm not sure they were actually trying to kill us. They kept wanting me to turn Joelle over to them, and while we were running, they probably had a chance or two to mow us down and didn't."

Until then, Joelle hadn't realized that. And maybe it didn't matter. Even though the gunmen might not have been trying to kill them, Dallas and she could have still been hit by one of those bullets.

"All hell's breaking loose back in town," Clayton said. "Owen's at the marshal's office claiming you kidnapped Joelle."

"I did," Dallas admitted at the same moment that Joelle answered, "He didn't."

Dallas looked at her and frowned.

"Someone drugged me," Joelle explained. "And Dallas removed me from the scene so he could question me and make sure I wasn't in danger."

Dallas's left eyebrow slid up.

"Owen already has enough to burn us," she mumbled. "I'm not giving him more."

Besides, she had to work out some kind of truce with Owen, and it wouldn't help any of them if Owen was hell-bent on arresting Dallas for kidnapping.

Dallas didn't take his attention off her. "Does this have something to do with the dirty little secret?"

"No," she snapped, but inside she was repeating, *Oh, God.* She couldn't deal with this now.

Clayton glanced at both of them, then at her engagement ring. "So, you're marrying Owen?" There was a boatload of suspicion and skepticism in his tone. "Never took you two for a love match. Always figured you'd end up with Dallas if he could ever forgive you for walking out on him."

"I don't forgive," Dallas grumbled. "And it's not a love match. Joelle's marrying the moron because he claims to have a knife with my prints and Webb's blood."

Joelle hadn't expected for Dallas just to blurt it out like that, but then she remembered this wasn't just his foster brother but a fellow marshal. He trusted Clayton. Heck, so did she.

To a point.

But neither of them was going to be able to defuse this Owen bomb. She could.

Well, maybe.

"She's marrying Owen to keep you from being arrested," Clayton concluded under his breath. "How'd your prints get on the knife?"

At least he hadn't asked if Dallas was guilty of murder. Maybe he didn't want to know. Or maybe he knew unequivocally that his foster brother was innocent.

Joelle certainly hadn't given Dallas the benefit of the doubt. And look where that had gotten her.

Dallas shook his head. "I'm sure I handled a knife or two during my time at Rocky Creek."

"Yeah, we all did," Clayton admitted. "I remember for a while there you kept one under your pillow when Webb was gunning so hard for Declan."

That brought the old memories flooding back. Joelle hadn't known about the knife, but she did know that Dallas and the others were often put in positions where they had to protect Declan. What Joelle had never understood was why Webb had had it in for Declan. And why Declan had never seemed to be able to back down even when Webb was basically assaulting him.

"You got a look at the knife?" Clayton asked, and it took a moment to realize he was talking to her.

Joelle nodded, but when she didn't say more, Dallas huffed. "If you know whose knife it is, now's the time to tell me."

It wasn't the time. Not with the adrenaline pumping through her and the drug hazing her mind. Still, he had to know. "It's a hunting knife with a black wood handle. It has one of those hooked tips."

Clayton and Dallas exchanged glances. "A gut hook," Dallas supplied. He didn't add more, but Joelle was certain that he recalled seeing a knife like that.

On Kirby.

His foster father had come to Rocky Creek a lot, and one time he'd taken the boys hunting. Joelle hadn't gone with them, but she remembered that knife, or one similar to it, in a leather sheath that Kirby had attached to his belt.

"A lot of people have knives like that," Dallas grumbled. And the silence settled uncomfortably between them.

"Saul's in the office with Owen," Clayton said a moment later.

Yet something else to make them uncomfortable. Saul Warner, Dallas's boss. Joelle had never met the man, but she figured it wasn't a good sign that the head marshal had been brought in on this. Of course, Owen would have seen to it. This was no doubt the beginning of the end.

Owen would bring Dallas down.

Her, too. And any of Dallas's foster family he could take with them.

Yes, Owen was guilty of criminal activity, but those charges wouldn't be nearly as serious as murder—unless they could connect Owen to those gunmen in the woods. Joelle was betting that wouldn't be easy to prove.

No.

Yet another reason why she had to work on a truce with Owen.

"Joelle needs to go to the hospital," Dallas said as they reached the edge of town.

"No. Go to the marshals' office." Owen already had the jump on them. Heck, he might even be working out some kind of *truce* with Saul Warner, and she didn't want to waste any time getting to him.

Dallas frowned. "I'll call the hospital and have them send a medic to do a blood test."

Good. Then maybe she could use the results to somehow rein in Owen. It wasn't as good as an incriminating knife, but it was something.

Clayton drove to the marshal's headquarters on Main Street and parked in the lot adjacent to the building. It was only when Joelle hurried out of the vehicle that she remembered she was wearing a robe and slippers. Hardly the attire for what would no doubt turn out to be an official interview, but there was no time to change.

A wave of dizziness came over her again as they crossed the parking lot, and like before, Dallas caught her arm. Supporting her. Just as he'd been doing for most of their ordeal. She couldn't let it continue. It'd be too easy to slip back into old ways and feelings. Best if she kept an emotional and physical distance, and that's why she moved away from him.

"I haven't forgotten," he grumbled. Her gaze flew to his. "About the *secret*," he added. "You will explain that to me later."

No, she wouldn't. But since it would only cause an argument or make him more suspicious to say that, Joelle kept quiet.

While they made their way up the stairs, Dallas called the hospital and requested a medic. He kept it short and sweet, which was a good thing because the moment they stepped into the marshals' office, she spotted Owen talking to the lanky fifty-something man.

Marshal Saul Warner.

Another of Dallas's foster brothers, Harlan McKinney, was there, as well. He, too, gave her an icy welcome, and all three turned toward Dallas, Clayton and her.

"Joelle," Owen said on a rush of breath. "You're okay." He hurried over to her and would have pulled her into his arms if Dallas hadn't stepped between them.

"She's okay, no thanks to you," Dallas challenged.

Joelle couldn't agree more. She wavered between being outraged that Owen had attempted to hug her and shocked as to why he would, but she tamped down both emotions.

"We have to talk," she told Owen. "In private." Groveling was a distinct possibility, but she needed to make sure Owen didn't blab anything to Marshal Warner.

"You can forget that *in private* request," Dallas snarled before turning to Owen. "You drugged Joelle."

Owen flinched. "What are you talking about?"

That earned him a groan from Dallas. "The Jack Daniel's that you sent to her dressing room was drugged, and you damn well know it."

"I didn't," he answered quickly. Owen cursed, shook his head and appeared as if he were trying to wrap his mind around something so impossible. "Wait." His gaze flew to Marshal Warner. "If someone drugged her, it was probably Lindsey Downing. She works for me and is Joelle's friend—"

"Yes, it was Lindsey," Joelle volunteered.

"Don't cover for him," Dallas warned her.

Joelle had to cover. There was no other choice here. "Lindsey could be jealous." And that was the truth. "I think she's in love with Owen."

Dallas gave her a flat look. "Then why the hell was she your bridesmaid?"

She wanted to postpone this explanation, but all four men had their full attention aimed at her. "The wedding was put together hastily. And Lindsey helped. It was too short notice for any of my friends to attend, so Lindsey asked if she could be in the wedding party." Besides, Joelle hadn't wanted her real friends to know what she was doing. Her plan had been to make the marriage as short as possible until she could get her hands on any and all evidence that would send Owen to jail without retaliation against her, Dallas or his family.

"What about the knife?" Marshal Warner asked.

Joelle could have sworn her stomach dropped to her knees. She looked at Owen, hoping and praying that the marshal meant some other knife, but Owen only gave her a smug glance.

The SOB. He'd ratted them out.

She silently cursed. "What about it?" she asked, not wanting to volunteer anything. She also hoped that Dallas wouldn't, either.

"What knife?" Harlan asked.

"It might be the weapon that killed Jonah Webb," Owen volunteered.

She gave Owen a look that she wished could have turned him to dust. Joelle could only stand there and brace herself for the worst.

"According to Mr. Palmer here," Warner said, "the

knife has some possible evidence that could link it to Jonah Webb's death."

Possible and *could.* So, Owen hadn't spilled all. Maybe because he thought he could still use it to control her. He definitely wanted to neutralize the possibility of her testifying against him.

Marshal Warner made a sound that could have meant anything, and the silence began again. Joelle waited for Dallas's boss to ask her about the test she'd had run. The test that had made her an accomplice in all of this. But he didn't say a word about it. Neither did Owen.

"How'd you get this knife?" Clayton asked Owen, and it wasn't a friendly request for information. Obviously, he disliked Owen as much as Dallas did.

"Someone sent it to me," Owen readily answered. "It was in a plastic bag inside a box with no return address, but postmarked from San Antonio."

Joelle glared at him. He'd told her that he'd found the knife in Webb's office, which meant he was lying then.

Or now.

Dallas glared, too. Shifted his position. Put his hands on his hips. "Any reason you didn't turn this knife over to the authorities the moment you got it?"

Owen lifted his shoulder. "I didn't realize what it was at the time. There was no note. No explanation. I put it in a safe-deposit box and was trying to find out who had sent it and why. Now, mind you, it wasn't a top priority since I was planning my wedding to Joelle."

"Right," Dallas said, his tone dripping with sarcasm. "Let me put that in my *I'm not buying it* file."

Owen ignored that and turned back to Marshal Warner. "Then yesterday I got another package. No return address again and also postmarked from San Antonio.

There was a typed note inside that said the traces of blood on the knife are Webb's and the prints belong to...Joelle."

Joelle couldn't stop the gasp that came from her mouth, but she clamped her teeth over her bottom lip so that she wouldn't blurt out that Owen had just told a whopper. She'd had the knife tested, and those were Dallas's prints.

Not hers.

Everything inside her was yelling for her to come clean with the head marshal. Not to clear her name but because Owen was weaving some kind of spider web here, and if she withheld info about the tests she'd run, she could be helping Owen with whatever stupid plan he was now concocting.

However, if she spoke up, she'd have to admit the tests she'd run. She'd have to admit that Dallas's prints were on the knife. She would also have to confess to withholding evidence in a murder case. She'd be arrested along with Dallas.

"Joelle didn't kill Webb," Dallas said before she could speak up, "so the knife must be a fake. Or else someone planted evidence on it."

"Possibly," Owen admitted, sounding smug again. "But that's why I'm turning it over to Marshal Warner here. I have someone retrieving it from the safe-deposit box as we speak." Owen looked at Joelle, obviously waiting to see how she'd respond.

"Then we'll wait for the test results," Dallas insisted, and he shot her a stay-quiet look.

She wanted to pull both Owen and him aside so she could try to do the right thing, but Dallas's iron gaze had her holding her tongue.

Joelle prayed that didn't turn out to be a big mistake.

Marshal Warner gave them each a considering look. "I'll accept custody of the knife and arrange for it to be sent to the lab. Since all of you were at Rocky Creek at the time of Webb's death, it's best if none of you has a part in this."

Owen quickly nodded, stepped closer to Joelle. "And while we're waiting for the results, Joelle and I can proceed with the marriage."

"What?" she blurted out.

"Not a chance," Dallas added. "She's been drugged, remember? A medic needs to check her. She'll need lab work. And we'll need to take yours and Lindsey's statements to figure out who put that drug in the drink."

Owen's eyes narrowed for just a split second, and then he must have remembered that Marshal Warner was watching his every move. "I hope you'll be questioned, too, about kidnapping her. That wasn't necessary, you know. I was already on the way to the church and could have handled the situation."

Again, Dallas stepped in front of her. "Your idea of handling it would have had her saying 'I do' even though she was drugged out of her mind."

Since this was quickly turning into an argument and because she was tired of having Dallas fight her battles, Joelle nudged him aside and faced Owen. "Dallas didn't think it was safe for me to be at the church and therefore he won't be questioned for *kidnapping*."

She tossed Dallas one of those stay-quiet glares he'd been giving her since this conversation had first started. "That doesn't mean I approve of what he did," she continued. "I could have gotten out of the church by myself."

Dallas made a yeah-right sound.

"This is all starting to sound personal," Marshal Warner interrupted. "Is it?"

Harlan and Clayton looked away, leaving it to her and Dallas to answer.

"Joelle used to have a thing for Dallas," Owen volunteered. "Old water, old bridge. She broke things off with him when she was a teenager, and she's my fiancée now. As far as I'm concerned, the wedding will take place ASAP, right after a doctor confirms she's okay, of course."

Even though that was an accurate summary, there was something in Owen's tone and expression. Maybe something about her dirty little secret.

Did Owen know?

Or was her guilty conscience coming in to play?

"Why don't we step into the hall and discuss this?" she said to Owen. Joelle didn't give him a chance to say no. She grabbed him by the arm and jerked him toward the door.

But the private conversation she'd intended suddenly wasn't so private because Dallas stepped into the hall with them and shut the door. Not that she could blame him. He had just as much stake in this as she did. Maybe more.

"What game are you playing now?" Joelle immediately asked Owen. She kept her voice to a whisper and glanced around to make sure no one was within hearing range. Thankfully, they had the hall to themselves.

"No game," Owen insisted. "I just want you to go through with our deal."

"Our deal was for you to keep the knife hidden away until I could prove who really murdered Webb. Now that you're turning it over to Marshal Warner, the deal is broken."

"Maybe not. It'll take a couple of days to get back the preliminary test results. A lot can go wrong during that time. The knife could be lost. Evidence could be destroyed."

Dallas groaned. "And that will only make me or some member of my family look guiltier."

"Not my problem." The smugness was so thick now that Joelle was afraid Dallas might slug Owen. She grabbed Dallas's arm so that he wouldn't move any closer to the man.

But the gesture clearly didn't have a good effect on Owen. He glanced at her grip on Dallas's arm. At their faces. At *them*. And his smugness turned to an ice-cold glare.

"This isn't finished," Owen said to Dallas. "If Joelle doesn't go through with the wedding, both of you are going down for Webb's murder. Kirby, too."

Dallas's jaw turned to iron. "What the hell does Kirby have to do with this?"

"Everything. There was a detailed account of how Kirby disposed of the body in the second package someone sent me. That makes him an accessory to murder, which carries the same penalty as murder itself."

Joelle's stomach churned again, but she forced herself to think. "I know the law, and I know you need proof. Some anonymous statement won't do it."

An oily smile tugged at Owen's mouth. "Oh, didn't I mention what else was in the package? Must have slipped my mind. The knife containing Webb's blood and your prints was wrapped in a handkerchief. Kirby's. And it has his DNA on it to prove it. All together, it looks like some kind of family effort to murder Webb. Throw in Joelle's obstruction of justice, and I see the three of you landing in jail."

"We won't be alone," Joelle snapped. "If we're arrested, I'll spill everything."

"Oh, yeah?" Owen countered. "Well, so will I."

She flinched, and the *oh, Gods* started to run through her head again.

"What's he talking about now?" Dallas demanded.

Joelle didn't answer. Couldn't. Suddenly, all the old memories came flooding back, and she couldn't speak over the lump in her throat.

Owen leaned in and pulled her grip off Dallas's arm. "I figure you've got a couple of days at most until that knife is processed and you're arrested. At any time Joelle can stop it by marrying me."

"I won't let Joelle marry you to save me," Dallas snarled.

Owen's smile flashed again. "No, but you would let her do it to save Kirby. Plus, there are things you don't know. Things Joelle wants to keep secret."

Now it was Dallas who stopped her from going after Owen. How dare he do this? But what had she expected? Joelle had known the man was a piece of work, but what she hadn't known was that he'd be able to get this kind of information.

"I will stop you," she warned him, though she didn't have a clue how to do that.

"Stop me?" Owen repeated. He stayed quiet a moment, but she couldn't tell from his expression what he was thinking. But it couldn't be good. "Then maybe you should speak with Kirby."

"Why?" Dallas asked immediately, and it sounded like a threat, warning Owen not to bring Kirby into this. On this point, Joelle agreed with Dallas. She didn't want Kirby any more involved than he already was.

"Kirby has a lot of answers," Owen finished seconds later. "But the question is—will he give them to you?"

"He's lying," Joelle said, hoping she was right.

"What answers?" Dallas pressed.

Another lift of his shoulder. "You should ask him."

"Kirby's sick," Joelle reminded Dallas, but he only made a sound to let her know he was still giving it some thought.

She wanted to throttle Owen again. There was no way Dallas would drop this now unless Kirby was genuinely too weak to talk with them. Joelle didn't want to benefit from the too-weak possibility, but she was afraid of what Kirby might say.

"Call me when you're ready to go through with the wedding," Owen said to her. He opened his mouth to say more, but the sound of footsteps stopped him.

Dallas and Joelle turned, and she spotted the man coming up the stairs. He was bald and bulky, and she recognized him as one of Owen's bodyguards who'd been at the church. He was carrying a package.

"Ah, the knife and other evidence are here." Owen threw open the door to the marshals' office where Clayton, Harlan and Chief Warner were all waiting.

Owen's bodyguard went inside with the package, but Owen stayed back, leaned in and put his mouth to Joelle's ear.

"Can you feel the seconds just ticking by?" he taunted in a whisper.

"Give me a week," Joelle pleaded.

But Owen just shook his head. "No deal."

"Don't even try to do this," Dallas warned her. "You're not marrying him."

Joelle ignored Dallas. Or rather, she tried to. It was hard to ignore him when he was right in her face.

"Give me three days then," she tried again with Owen.

Another headshake. Another smile. "You've got forty-eight hours to marry me, that's all," Owen insisted. "Then all hell will break loose, and I'll tell Dallas *everything*."

Chapter Seven

"You sure Kirby's up to this?" Joelle asked again.

"Yeah," Dallas lied.

Kirby was in no shape to be answering questions about Webb's murder, the knife or anything else, but Dallas knew that his foster father would do it anyway. Kirby would do anything humanly possible to keep any of them from being arrested for the murder of a man who hadn't deserved to live.

Joelle blew out a deep breath and continued leaning her head against the passenger's window of his truck. It's where she'd been leaning it since they'd started the drive from Maverick Springs to his family's ranch. She'd moved briefly just to hurry inside her hotel room so she could collect her things and change into a skirt and a top.

Better than that peekaboo bathrobe.

She was clearly exhausted, probably hungover from the drugs and the adrenaline crash, but she was nervous, too. Nibbling on her bottom lip and mumbling something about Owen. There wasn't time for her to rest or even compose herself. Dallas hated to admit it, but with time eating away, he needed all the help he could get.

Especially Joelle's.

She'd already spent weeks looking into Webb's murder, and it would waste time they didn't have for him to go back and recreate what she'd managed to get done. They needed answers, and they needed them fast.

Dallas's phone rang just as he took the final turn toward Blue Creek ranch. He saw on the screen that the caller was Clayton, probably with an update on what was happening, so he put the call on speaker since Joelle would no doubt want to hear.

"Please tell me you found the gunmen," Dallas greeted. Because if they found them and tied them back to Owen, they could discredit Owen and the evidence that he'd turned over to Saul Warner.

"Still looking," Clayton said. "But I thought you'd want to know that Lindsey Downing is here and claiming she had no part in drugging Joelle."

"She's lying," Joelle immediately said.

"Probably," Clayton continued, "but she's saying that she merely poured you a drink from the bottle that was in the reception room at the church."

"She claims there was a bottle of booze just lying around?" Dallas pressed.

"Yep."

Hell. Dallas wanted to drive back to headquarters and question the woman himself. He could threaten the truth out of her. But he wouldn't be able to get in the front door.

Saul's orders.

Dallas couldn't blame his boss for excluding not just him but all five of his foster brothers from this particular investigation. Having them involved was the textbook definition of conflict of interest. Still, that wouldn't stop all of them from finding the truth on their own. Even Saul couldn't fault them for that.

The family was at stake.

"What about the knife?" Dallas asked Clayton. "What did Saul do with it?"

"He's arranged to have it couriered over to the lab in a few hours. And before you ask, he won't delay it until tomorrow. He said everything's got to be aboveboard on this and that with all the interviews he's doing, two hours is a reasonable amount of time for him to do the lab paperwork."

Yeah, it did have to be aboveboard because Owen would jump to report them to the governor, the rangers or the FBI if they did anything out of the ordinary. Of course, if Owen did that, he'd also have to explain why he'd withheld potential evidence even for this period of time.

"I figure we've got three days at most before the preliminary results are back," Clayton continued.

Joelle groaned softly. Owen had only given her two days. Hardly enough time to even find a starting point for the rest of the investigation. And that's why Dallas had had no choice but to turn to Kirby, and he prayed like the devil that his father had a reasonable explanation for that handkerchief wrapped around the knife. While he was praying, he needed to come up with his legal, plausible reason as to why his prints were on a possible murder weapon.

Yeah, they needed a boatload more time.

"Whatever Kirby tells us, we'll go from there," Dallas assured his brother. "And call me as soon as Joelle's lab results are in."

With that reminder, she glanced down at the crook of her arm, peeled off the bandage that the medic had put in place after drawing a blood sample and pinched the bandage into a little ball. Almost as if she were trying to work out her anger with the motion.

It wouldn't help.

Joelle probably felt violated. And had been. Now the

question was—who was responsible? His money was still on Owen using Lindsey as a lackey, but proving Owen's guilt was the next step.

"What about the other woman who was at the church with Lindsey?" Dallas asked Clayton. "Has she been brought in yet?"

"Amanda Mathis," Joelle interjected.

"She's on her way," Clayton answered. "I'll try to hang around to hear what she has to say, but Saul is already trying to boot me out the door. Harlan, too. And he's already sent Slade and Wyatt to prisoner transport duty."

Again, not unexpected but a damn inconvenience. Working from the inside out would be a heck of a lot easier than the reverse. Of course, both of those scenarios involved working with Joelle. Not his first choice of investigative partners. Too much old blood between them. Old wounds, too.

And apparently remnants of the attraction.

Nothing would come of it. Dallas was sure of that. He needed his head on this case and not clouded with memories of kisses and sex.

"You still there, Dallas?" Clayton asked.

Dallas snapped his attention back to the conversation and cursed the clouded head he already had.

"Hang in there as long as you can," Dallas instructed Clayton, and he ended the call.

"Amanda wouldn't have done this," Joelle volunteered right away. "She also works for Owen, but unlike Lindsey, she's a mouse. If he gave the order to one of them, it would have been Lindsey."

Dallas thought about that while he pulled to a stop in front of the sprawling ranch house. However, he didn't get out, and Joelle didn't seem so anxious to do that, either.

"Would Lindsey have done this on her own, without Owen's order?" Dallas asked.

She paused. "Maybe. Probably," Joelle amended a moment later. "I believe she's in love with Owen so who knows—this might have been her way of stopping the ceremony."

"Does Lindsey know that Owen forced you into this engagement?"

Joelle shook her head. "I doubt Owen shared that with anyone. He would want everyone to believe that I'm marrying him for love."

Good point. Yeah, Owen's ego would have insisted on that. "Could Lindsey have been the one to hire those men in the woods?"

Joelle blinked. "Why wouldn't you believe Owen did that?"

"I do think it was him, but I have to look at this the way my boss will. And Saul will want to know if there was someone other than Owen with means, motive and opportunity to drug you and send out those gunmen."

She made a sound of agreement, then groaned. "Lindsey fits the bill on all counts. She comes from a wealthy family so she'd have the funds to hire gunmen. She's also in love with Owen. And hates me. She could have called the goons as soon as you took me out of the church." But then, Joelle shook her head. "Still, it all goes back to Owen. I mean, why would Lindsey want those men to force me back to the church?"

Unfortunately, Dallas could think of a reason. "Maybe they weren't instructed to take you to the church. Maybe they were hired to make sure you never married Owen."

And if so, perhaps they really had orders to kill her.

Of course, there was that part about a dirty little secret. Dallas wanted to ask Joelle if Lindsey would have known anything about that. Or had Owen known? But Joelle had made it pretty clear that particular subject wasn't up for discussion.

Not now, anyway.

But soon, very soon, Dallas would need to hear it in case it was somehow connected to this mess of an investigation.

"Owen certainly had the means to hire those men," Joelle continued. "And more."

Yeah. Dallas was aware of that. Right after he'd finished college, Owen had married the only daughter of one of the richest ranchers in Texas, and both father and daughter had died in a car accident less than a year later. As the sole heir, Owen had inherited the successful ranch along with about twenty million dollars.

That could buy a lot of gunmen.

"You've stayed in touch with Owen all these years?" he asked.

"No." A quick answer, and she made a face as if the idea was an unpleasant one. "He's called a time or two and dropped by my office once, but I was never interested in seeing or hearing from Owen."

"Yet he found a way to tangle you in his life." And tangle in a bad way. In addition to the dirty little secret conversation, Dallas would need to see the evidence Joelle had found that would incriminate the piece of scum who was blackmailing her into marriage.

"It's a nice place," Joelle said when Dallas opened his truck door.

Dallas followed her gaze to the white limestone house. It wasn't a new structure. The ranch had been in Kirby's family for six generations.

"Most people just describe it as *big*," he mumbled. And it seemed to be constantly growing. After Kirby had taken him and his five foster brothers in, he'd added a second floor and expanded the kitchen and living areas.

Joelle got out slowly, and even though she was no longer wobbling when she walked, her steps were tentative. "I'm still not sure this is a good idea."

Before Dallas could remind her again that they were short on options, the front door opened and Declan stepped onto the porch that stretched across the entire front of the house.

"Joelle," Declan greeted. He said her name with some disdain. No doubt because of her inquiry that could ultimately burn Kirby.

Dallas frowned, grabbed her overnight bag and joined them. Joelle looked a little hurt by Declan's frosty welcome, and there was good reason for that. Back at Rocky Creek, she and Declan had always been friendly in a big sister, little brother kind of way. But Dallas really didn't want her welcomed back with open arms.

"You look good," Joelle said to Declan. "I've missed you."

That didn't sit well with Dallas, either, and he didn't take the bark out of his tone. "We have to talk to Kirby," he said as he put her bag on the entry floor and pulled off his Stetson. He hung it on its usual hook next to the door.

"Yeah," Declan acknowledged. "Clayton called and filled me in. Kirby knows, too."

"And he's up to seeing us?" Joelle asked.

Declan shook his head and tipped his head for her to follow him inside. "Not really up to it, but he insisted on the visit."

"Then we'll keep it short," she promised.

Declan started toward Kirby's bedroom at the back of the house. "Is Joelle staying the night?"

"No," she answered, probably because she felt about as welcome as the flu.

"Yes," Dallas contradicted. "Until those gunmen are found, she's staying with one of us."

Declan didn't argue with him, though Dallas thought Joelle might.

"I'll have Loretta fix up the guest room," his brother commented. "Loretta's our housekeeper," Declan added, glancing back at Joelle.

"Loretta Wiggins," she said as they wound their way through the hall.

"You know her?" Dallas asked, surprised.

Joelle nodded. "When the governor asked me to look into Webb's death, I asked for background checks on all of you, including your help here at the ranch."

It made him wonder what else she'd done. And learned. She certainly hadn't learned anything from his immediate family firsthand but had instead sent her assistant, a pasty-faced lawyer, to interview him and his foster brothers. Maybe because Joelle hadn't wanted to personally confront what she thought would be a bunch of riled lawmen.

Or maybe she just hadn't wanted to confront *him*.

They stopped in front of Kirby's door, and Declan looked at them. "He's been out of it most of the day. Asking for Stella again."

"Stella Doyle?" Joelle immediately asked. "The cook who was at Rocky Creek?"

Declan nodded, then scratched his head. "Didn't even realize Kirby and Stella knew each other that well, but he wants to see her."

"One of my people interviewed her," Joelle offered. "I'm sure we have current contact information."

Dallas huffed. He already had too much on his plate,

but if Kirby wanted the woman to come to the ranch, he'd figure out a way to get her there. As long as Kirby didn't want to see Stella for some deathbed farewell, that is. He didn't want Kirby giving up on the treatments.

When Dallas reached for the doorknob, Joelle took several deeps breaths. She opened her mouth, probably to repeat that this wasn't a good idea, but Dallas opened the door anyway. And there Kirby was on the bed.

Hell.

He looked worse than he had earlier when Dallas left for the church to stop Joelle's wedding. Kirby opened his eyes. Not without some effort. And he turned his head in their direction. He even managed a watery smile for Joelle's benefit.

God, it hurt to see him like this. Kirby had always been so strong. A hulk of a man. And now the cancer and the treatments had reduced him to practically a skeleton.

"I'll get Loretta started on that guest room," Declan said, excusing himself.

Kirby lifted his hand and motioned for them to come closer. "Tell me about Owen," he mumbled, and his hand eased back onto the bed.

Dallas wanted to keep this as short as possible because he knew even a simple conversation would be exhausting for Kirby. "Owen claims someone sent him a knife containing Webb's blood and my prints and that it was wrapped in your handkerchief. He just turned it over to Saul, who's sending it to the lab."

"Owen always was a wormy little snake," Kirby mumbled.

That wasn't exactly what Dallas wanted to hear. He'd wanted Kirby to say the evidence had to be fake, that there was no way his handkerchief could be wrapped around a murder weapon.

"Saul wouldn't let me look at the knife," Dallas continued. "He wants me to stay away from all of this." He motioned to Joelle. "But she had it tested, and they're apparently my prints."

"Dallas could have handled that knife at any time," Joelle said, her voice a whisper. "And Webb's killer could have used gloves during the murder so that only Dallas's prints were the ones on it."

She stayed back from Kirby's bed and dodged his gaze when he turned his head in her direction.

What the heck was going on?

Maybe the idea of a dying man bothered her. Well, it bothered him, too, especially when that man was the only father Dallas had ever known.

"Owen's setting you up?" Kirby asked, his voice already so weak that it barely had any sound.

Joelle nodded.

"He's blackmailing Joelle to marry him," Dallas explained when she didn't say anything. "That won't stop the knife from being processed."

Or stop Dallas and maybe others from being arrested.

He walked closer to Kirby. "Look, I know you're not well enough to leave town, but I want to hire you a good lawyer. One who'll make sure that no one tries to include you in this mess."

The corner of Kirby's mouth lifted. "You're a good son, Dallas. But let the chips fall where they may."

"What the hell does that mean?" Dallas snapped. "I'm not letting them arrest you, especially for something you didn't do."

Again, Kirby didn't jump to say he was innocent, but Dallas didn't care. Jonah Webb had been a scum of a man, and no one should be going to jail for stopping him. Especially Kirby.

"You need to go back to Rocky Creek," Kirby said several moments later. "Talk with the people who were there the night that Webb disappeared. Look around and see what you can find."

"Joelle and her people have already done that," Dallas reminded him. But Dallas did intend to examine all of her notes and statements.

"No," Kirby said. "You and Joelle go. *You* talk to them. You look for something that others may have missed." He drew in a labored breath. "I don't know what answers you'll find there, but you'll find something."

Yeah. But he damn sure didn't want to find anything to corroborate that knife and handkerchief.

Kirby lifted his hand again, pointed at Joelle and motioned for her to come closer. She froze for just a split second. But Dallas definitely noticed. He also didn't miss the uneasy look in her eyes.

Yeah. Something was definitely going on here.

Dallas waited. Watched and listened. Joelle inched her way to Kirby's bed. When she was close enough, Kirby reached out and took her hand.

"You have to tell him," Kirby said. "Dallas needs to know."

"Know what?" Dallas immediately asked.

Joelle shook her head, and now she dodged Dallas's gaze.

"Yes," Kirby insisted. "Tell him. No more secrets."

Secrets. There it was again. That blasted word that Dallas was beginning to hate. One of the gunmen in the woods had said something about a secret, and Joelle hadn't brushed it off.

Well, she wouldn't brush it off now.

Dallas took her arm and led her back to the hall so they could talk in private.

"Go easy on her," Kirby mumbled. "Everything she's done is because she's still in love with you. Even a dying man can see that."

Dallas cursed. In this case the dying man was wrong. The only thing Dallas saw when he looked at Joelle was a woman who'd abandoned him sixteen years ago. She wasn't keeping secrets for love; she was keeping them, well, he didn't know why.

Yet.

Dallas practically dragged her from the room, and when he shut Kirby's door, he got right in her face.

"Start talking," Dallas demanded. And this time, he wasn't taking no for an answer.

Chapter Eight

It was too late for Joelle to try and duck around Dallas. He backed her against the wall and pinned her in place with his body. Despite all the things going through her head, she still noticed the close contact.

His chest pressed against her breasts.

Dallas obviously noticed it, too, because he glanced down between them and then stepped back a little. "That won't get you off the hook," he mumbled.

"That?" she blurted out. Yet another bad idea. She should have just dropped the subject completely.

"You know what I'm talking about." He didn't wait for her to confirm that yep, she did know. It was this blasted attraction between them. "It won't play into this. You'll tell me all about this secret you've been keeping."

She would. No way around it now. Joelle debated where to start, but before she could figure out a jumping off point, she heard the footsteps, and Declan appeared in the hall.

"The guest room's ready," he said, and his gaze slid to the still close contact between Dallas and her. "Looks like old times." Declan didn't exactly seemed pleased about that, either.

Dallas cursed. "Mind your own business. And if you remember correctly, those old times weren't always good." But he stepped away from her again. "Come on. We'll have this discussion in private."

He was right. Kirby had been stressed out enough without having to listen to them argue. And there would be an argument if she didn't tell all. The trick was to do that without making things worse.

Latching on to her arm again, Dallas scowled at her and then led her down the hall and into what she assumed was the guest room. Her bag sat near the bed.

"Talk," Dallas ordered.

Joelle gathered her breath first. It wasn't easy, and even when she managed to do it, it didn't help. "One of the first things I discovered when I started this inquiry was that neither you, Kirby nor any of your foster brothers have foolproof alibis for the time Webb went missing."

"Not exactly a secret," Dallas pointed out.

"No. But my boss was pressing me to name some top suspects, preferably not any state officials or employees with ties to Rocky Creek."

Dallas stayed quiet a moment. Cursed again. "He wants to pin this on a federal marshal."

"Only if a marshal is guilty," she corrected. "This isn't a witch hunt, Dallas. The governor wants everything aboveboard, but he wants it handled discreetly, too. And that's why I didn't interview you or your brothers personally. I didn't want anyone to think that I'd manipulated or influenced your accounts of that night."

"So you sent a lackey to talk to us."

"My assistant," she corrected. "And I used the info from those interviews and others to come up with a timetable of who was where and when for all sixty-one residents and the staff."

He stared at her. "You found something." And it wasn't a question.

"I found that the time window was short for you to have committed a murder, but it was still possible." She had to swallow hard and tried not to allow the images of that night into her head. "Webb was last seen at eight in the evening, and you met me by the creek at eight-thirty. I didn't want to put in my report that you could have murdered Webb and then calmly had sex with me."

"Calmly?" he questioned. "We never did anything *calmly,* especially sex."

Joelle couldn't help it, she smiled and then had to choke back a laugh. Why, she didn't know. There was certainly nothing laughable about any of this. Including those memories. But Dallas was right once again—when they'd been together in those days, it'd been anything but calm.

The images came so fast, so hard that Joelle couldn't push them all away. Sixteen years was a long time, but for some reason her brain and body just wouldn't let her forget Dallas's touch. His scent. His taste.

It was always there with her.

"Yeah," Dallas mumbled, and the corner of his mouth lifted as if he were about to smile. He didn't. The moment came and went, and the steel returned to his eyes.

With reason.

He was never going to forgive her for leaving him, and part of Joelle would never forgive herself. No use going back down that road because reliving it would only make matters worse.

"The timeline," she said, hoping to get her own mind back where it belonged—on this investigation. "You aren't the only one with a short window for an alibi. Eyewitnesses put Harlan and Clayton in their room around eight-fifteen. Slade was unloading boxes in the kitchen about that time. Wyatt was apparently in one of the storage sheds making out with Amy Simmons, the caretaker's daughter."

Dallas nodded, probably because he remembered Wyatt's string of hot and heavy romances. It seemed that Wyatt had grown up a lot faster than the rest of them had, and his rock-star cowboy looks hadn't hurt one bit. Back then, anyway. Wyatt was the only one of them to have ever married. Of course, that hadn't worked out so well for him. His wife had died two years ago, and he hadn't put those rock-star looks to use by jumping back into the dating pool.

"That leaves Declan," Dallas finally said, "and he was in the infirmary because Webb had given him a beating just hours earlier."

Now, it was her turn to nod. "But no one can verify that Declan was actually there."

Dallas's next round of profanity was raw. "Declan was barely thirteen and scrawny. No way could he have stabbed a man Webb's size."

"I agree. But he could have gotten the drop on him and surprised him. Declan had a strong motive. And he threatened to kill Webb when he beat him."

"Hell, I threatened Webb, too." Dallas groaned, put his hands on his hips. "This sure as hell better not be the secret—that you're going to tell the governor that Declan is the killer."

"No." And that's all she said for several seconds. "A few weeks ago, Kirby called me and said he had proof that he'd murdered Webb."

"He didn't!" Dallas shouted.

Since Dallas looked on the verge of exploding, she hurried toward him and took him by the arm to keep him from storming back to Kirby's room for an explanation.

"I don't believe Kirby killed Webb, either," Joelle said, blocking Dallas's path.

Another bad idea. Because they slammed into each other again. She still wasn't too steady on her feet, and she stumbled. Right into Dallas's arms.

Instant contact again. Instant memories.

Instant heat, too.

She had to take a moment before she could continue. "I think whatever proof that Kirby claimed he had was fake. Or circumstantial at best. He was adamant that if it came down to one of you being arrested, that I would help him release the so-called evidence so that he'd be charged instead."

Dallas froze, obviously thinking about that. "You agreed to that stupid plan?"

"No. Because I knew none of you would allow it. But Dallas, I'm betting if one of you is arrested, whatever Kirby has will show up in some law enforcement office. And if he doesn't actually have anything, he might try to create it."

He didn't argue with that because he no doubt knew it was true. Joelle also figured it would be impossible to talk Kirby out of it. Even though until this incident she'd been out of touch with him for years, the man had always been a little pigheaded. And a lot pigheaded when it came to his foster sons.

Dallas again noticed the close contact between them and he moved away from her. Not far though. In fact, they ended up leaning against the same wall. Practically shoulder to shoulder.

"What specific evidence did Kirby say he had?" Dallas asked. He blew out a long breath and scrubbed his hand over his face.

"He didn't. But when Owen told me he had the knife,

I thought maybe he'd stolen it from Kirby. Kirby denied that."

"You and Kirby have been having a lot of conversations," he grumbled.

"Not long ones, I assure you. I know how sick he is, and I didn't press him on anything. In fact, I didn't want anyone to know about what he told me."

"A secret," Dallas repeated in the same tone as his profanity. "How did Owen find out?"

She blinked, and Joelle could have sworn her heart skipped a beat.

"Owen said you had secrets," Dallas clarified. "How did he find out this possible package of evidence that Kirby has?"

"I'm not sure," she answered as soon as she got her mouth working. "Maybe he bugged my condo. Maybe Lindsey did."

Oh, mercy.

With everything else going on, she hadn't considered that until now. Of course, either Lindsey or Owen was capable of doing something like that. Especially Owen. He would have definitely wanted to learn everything she'd found out about him.

"What exactly do you have on Owen that would make him go to these extremes?" Dallas asked.

Finally, an easy question, but she doubted he'd like this answer any more than the others she'd given him. "Investments with shady businesses, and Owen wasn't an innocent party in this, either. I believe it amounts to loan sharking."

Dallas groaned. "Doesn't sound like it's enough to put him away for a long time." He glanced at her and frowned. "Maybe all of his talk of you marrying him so you can't testify was a ruse on his part just to get you to the altar."

She opened her mouth to deny it, but then rethought it.

"Owen's always been hot for you," Dallas continued. "Heck, he could have set this all up. Everything. Including the evidence against him. You're sure what you have is solid enough to put him behind bars?"

Well, she had been until now. "It was one of Owen's former business associates who tipped me off about the illegal deals. I dug around, found some papers to corroborate the tip." She had to pause. "But someone broke into my office and stole the papers."

"Owen," Dallas quickly concluded.

Joelle had to nod. "Probably. I tried to get duplicates of everything that was stolen, but they, too, had been destroyed. And the tipster suddenly had to leave town."

"Damn, when Owen does a cover-up, he doesn't do it halfway," Dallas mumbled.

"Yes, except for me. I'm the loose end because I saw the documents and can testify that I did." She huffed. "Well, I can once Owen is no longer capable of putting us in jail."

"Neutralizing Owen is a must." Dallas pushed himself away from the wall and faced her. "I need to discredit him any way I can so it'll also discredit that knife and handkerchief. It'd be even better if I could find something to prove he murdered Webb."

Joelle wasn't sure that was possible, but with so much at stake, she would definitely try. "One problem is that Owen has a better alibi than any of you for the time of Webb's disappearance. He was with the caretaker, Rudy Simmons, from about seven to ten o'clock, and Rudy verifies it."

Dallas lifted his shoulder. "Maybe both are lying."

"I wish, and I wish I could prove it." And she'd tried to find a witness, anyone, who could dispute that time frame. But the bottom line was that Rudy simply didn't have a motive for murder.

Well, not one that she'd been able to find, anyway.

On the surface, Webb and he had actually been friends of sorts even though Webb was Rudy's boss.

"Owen is for starters," Dallas said, "but we need more. I don't believe any of my foster brothers or Kirby had a thing to do with Webb's death."

But he didn't sound convinced of that. Neither was Joelle.

"We have to name some other suspects," he added. "Credible ones, so we can end this investigation and clear our names."

Joelle couldn't argue with that. "Then we'll find them at Rocky Creek just as Kirby suggested. Jonah Webb's wife, Sarah, still lives on the grounds. Rudy Simmons does, too."

"What about Rudy's daughter, Amy, the one Wyatt was fooling around with in the shed?"

She had to shake her head. "She died a few years ago from leukemia. But even if she were alive, I doubt she'd make a good suspect. She was a lot smaller than Declan, and from what I can tell, she didn't have a motive."

In other words, Webb hadn't mentally and physically abused her the way he had some of the boys—like Dallas and Declan.

Dallas stayed quiet for a moment, then snapped his fingers. "Jonah and Sarah had a son, Billy. He was about fifteen when his father disappeared. What did he have to say about Webb's murder?"

Another headshake. "I couldn't find him." And she'd

tried hard. "But I do know he spent some time in a mental facility after an attempted suicide."

"Probably because his father used to beat the hell of him." Dallas nodded. "Yeah, definitely a motive for murder, and he was big enough to help kill a man. I'll see if my brothers can track him down."

Joelle wasn't about to refuse their help, not with Owen's ultimatum and the lab test hanging over their heads.

She was so involved in her thoughts that it took a moment for her to realize that Dallas was staring at her. And he was still too close. She started to move away, but he snagged her by the wrist.

"You're keeping something from me," he accused.

Joelle opened her mouth to deny that, but she didn't manage to get out a word.

"Or maybe you're just trying to hide the obvious," Dallas interrupted.

Unfortunately, she knew exactly what obvious he meant.

He got in her face. "This attraction won't affect what we have to do. In fact, it won't affect anything. Because we're going to pretend that it doesn't exist."

She rolled her eyes. "Oh, that helps a lot." Her stare dared him to disagree with her sarcasm.

He couldn't.

The air was practically sizzling between them, and it didn't cool down when they moved away from each other.

"So we don't pretend," he insisted. "We don't do anything about it." Then he cursed a blue streak.

"Denial's a pretty sucky deterrent, huh?"

"Yeah." And he just kept staring at her. Definitely didn't back away. But then, neither did she. So yes, denial wasn't going to stop this.

Maybe nothing would.

"I'm trying hard to remember why this can't happen," he mumbled a split second before he hooked his arm around her waist and snapped her to him.

It happened so fast that Joelle tried to brace herself for a kiss. But no bracing was necessary. Dallas moved his mouth toward hers. But he didn't kiss her. He didn't touch her with those lips that had kissed her too many times to count.

She could feel those old make-out sessions blood deep, and they sent a coil of heat from her head to her toes. Mercy. What was it about Dallas that turned her to mush? It wasn't fair that he would still have her hormonal number after all these years.

Cursing, he moved in even closer. Almost touching. So close that she took in his scent, and the coil of heat turned to a throbbing ache.

"Tell me why this is a bad idea," he growled. He slid his hand around the back of her neck, angling her head. Angling her body, too, with the grip he still had on her waist. They were pressed against each other like lovers now.

"Because you can't forgive me?" she said. "Because you hate me?"

He was right in her face, and she saw what she was saying register in his eyes. Both were valid reasons. Well, the first one, anyway. That didn't look like hate in all those swirls of blue. No hate in his body, either. His breath was uneven. Heart racing.

"Because we don't have time for this," Joelle tried again. "And because you'd regret it."

Dallas kept staring for what seemed an eternity, and even though he didn't move, her body seemed to think it was about to get lucky. Everything inside her was melting, urging her to do what Dallas had so far resisted.

Like kiss him.

"I would regret it," he finally said.

The breath swooshed out of her, and Joelle knew she should feel relief, but that damn ache in her body was overriding common sense. Yes, Dallas would regret it all right. And once the pleasure had worn off—and there would be pleasure—she would regret it, too.

Dallas cursed again. He squeezed his eyes shut a moment, then added a few more words of profanity.

"Get some rest," he snarled, and moved her aside so he could open the door. "First thing in the morning, we're going back to that hellhole at Rocky Creek, and one way or another we *will* find answers."

He headed out but then stopped when his phone beeped. With his back still to her, Dallas glanced at the screen and then groaned.

"What's wrong now?" Joelle immediately asked, praying that nothing else had happened.

No such luck.

"My boss just got orders from his supervisor to have the tests expedited on the knife and handkerchief." Dallas shook his head, then mumbled something she didn't catch. "They might have the preliminary results back as early as tomorrow."

"Tomorrow?" Oh, God.

"Yeah." He said the rest of what he had to say from over his shoulder. "We've got less than twenty-fours to clear Kirby's and our names, or Saul will have to arrest us."

Chapter Nine

The moment Dallas took the final turn onto the rural road, he spotted the place. Rocky Creek Children's Facility. He felt a punch of dread from the old memories, but he reminded himself that this visit was necessary.

So was Joelle.

Well, necessary for him to be able to speed through this investigation, anyway. But the sooner he put some distance between them, the better.

Joelle ducked down a little, probably so she could dodge the bright morning sunlight and take in the grounds and buildings. Even though he knew she'd recently visited the place, she seemed to shudder.

"It never did look like a prison," she mumbled.

No. But that's pretty much what it'd been since the kids sent there literally had had no other place to go and couldn't leave. In his case, it'd been because his druggie mother had abandoned him at a sheriff's office when he was seven, and since she wasn't even sure who his father was, that hadn't been an option. When Dallas hadn't been a good fit and a troublemaker to boot in the half-dozen foster homes where he'd been sent, he'd ended up in reform school. After that, Rocky Creek became a place of last resort.

And his home.

That *H* word obviously didn't have the same warm, fuzzy memories that it did for other kids, but reform school, Rocky Creek and his abandoning mother hadn't broken him. His past had actually given him the drive to make something better of himself.

Apparently, it'd done the same for Joelle, though she'd been placed there for a different kind of abandonment. When her parents had been killed in a car accident, they'd left provisions in their will for her to be taken to Rocky Creek because a relative worked there. Of course, by the time Joelle had arrived, the relative had been long gone, and she'd been on her own.

Until they'd found each other, that is.

"You okay?" Joelle asked him.

He hadn't realized she was staring at him, obviously noting his less than happy expression. "Yeah." And that wasn't a lie. "You?"

No *yeah* from her. "I just want to finish this."

He was on the same page with her when it came to that.

Dallas pulled to a stop in the driveway in front of the entrance of the sprawling redbrick building. The grounds were in good shape. The trees were all trimmed. The flower beds were weed-free. He'd expected to see the place in total disrepair, but it looked pretty much the same as it had sixteen years ago.

"Rudy and Sarah still take care of the place?" he asked.

"Yes. Rudy does the grounds. And Sarah cleans the place—often, from the looks of it. Well, she did before her husband's body was found and the inquiry started. After that, the state had the doors locked."

It made sense. Basic precautions had to be taken in case there was any evidence left inside, and it was a plenty big enough place for there to be some hidden evidence.

He hoped so, anyway.

Dallas stepped from his truck. Looked around. Not just at the facility but at the wooded area and grounds. He was certain no one had followed them, but their attackers were still at large so he had to take precautions.

Joelle got out as well and had her own look around. She wobbled a little on the pebbled drive and had to catch on to the truck to steady herself while she raked a small rock from her high heel.

"Not exactly the best shoes for a trek like this," he mumbled.

Or for keeping his attention off her. He could say the same for the entire outfit. A pale blue skirt and top that seemed to skim every curve of her body, and she had some curves, all right. The heels didn't help, either. They weren't exactly high, but they showed off her legs.

Yet something else that he'd always admired.

"The shoes and two similar outfits were all I'd brought with me," she explained. "I hadn't packed for an investigation."

No. She'd packed for a honeymoon. Dallas's stomach clenched at the thought of her wearing that outfit for Owen. Or wearing anything for him for that matter. Heck, his stomach clenched more at the thought of Owen looking at her while she was wearing nothing.

Oh, man.

He was a lost cause, and he forced his brain to dwell on something other than the shape of Joelle's butt.

Dallas cleared his throat, hoping it would also clear his head, and he walked up the steps. "I'm surprised the state hasn't torn the place down by now."

"They can't. The man who donated it back in the fifties put a stipulation in his will that it couldn't be removed, only renovated. So far, no one seems eager to do that, and the state doesn't have the desire or the money."

Because places like this were dinosaurs, thank God.

"Sarah's and Rudy's salaries are paid from the donor's estate," she added. "I guess that's one of the reasons they stay on."

It'd take a heck of a lot more than a paycheck for Dallas to continue to live here.

Joelle fished through the laptop bag she'd brought with her and came out with the keys to open the padlock on the metal bar latch that stretched across the double front doors.

"Where'd you get the keys?" Dallas asked.

"The governor's office."

They stepped inside, and Dallas looked around. Bare floors and walls. Not a stick of furniture in sight. But it was indeed clean. Sarah and Rudy had obviously taken their maintenance duties seriously.

"The furnishings were sold years ago," Joelle explained, "and the bulk of the records were moved to Austin when the place shut down, but there are still storage sheds. And Webb's office."

"Anything in there?" he asked.

"Plenty. It had been sealed off since the closure, and even Rudy and Sarah weren't given keys to the lock. It still has some of Webb's personal files, and it's where I spent most of my time when I first started the inquiry."

Dallas had no doubt she'd done a thorough job, too. "Anything left there to find?"

She lifted her shoulder and headed for the stairs. "Maybe you'll see something I missed. Then we can walk over to Sarah Webb's cottage and talk to her. Rudy lives in a trailer near the creek."

They went up the steps that Dallas had walked hundreds of time, and while his mind should have been solely on this visit, it wasn't. Damn his body. Certain parts of it, anyway. Those parts wouldn't let him forget this blasted attraction for Joelle.

"I need to apologize for what happened last night," he said.

She stopped in front of Webb's office and proceeded to open a padlock on yet another bar lock across the door. "Nothing happened."

He lifted his eyebrow.

"Nothing we can't ignore," she amended.

He wasn't so sure of that. There was something else he couldn't ignore, either. "I never have thanked you for trying to help Kirby and me."

"No need for thanks. I was helping myself, too. Or so I thought." She paused. "If I can't stop Owen, we're going to jail."

"It's not over until it's over." He hadn't meant that to sound, well, sexual, but it did. Or maybe that was just his blasted imagination.

Nope.

The slight quiver of Joelle's mouth let him know she was having similar thoughts, and that made both of them stupid.

She threw open the door, and though Dallas had thought he was prepared to see his old nemesis's office, he wasn't. A jolt of a different kind.

Webb had beaten him in this office.

Not just hours before Webb's disappearance but plenty of other times, too. And not just him but Declan and Harlan. Hell, the man had even slapped Joelle, and it didn't matter how many years had passed, that still put some acid in his gut.

Joelle shuddered again, maybe reliving the same memory. He saw the steel return to her eyes, and she plopped her bag on Webb's desk.

"I have a portable scanner," she explained, "and I copied things that I thought might be important." She pulled a handful of files from the desk drawer she'd unlocked, put them on the desk and unlocked the other drawers. "Like Webb's personal notes about the kids."

That grabbed his attention, and Dallas dropped down in the chair to have a better look. "He kept files on all of us?" He looked at the sheer number of folders that she was pulling from the drawers.

"Most of us." She plucked one from the stash and handed it to him. It was his file. "I went through all of them, looking for a motive for Webb's murder."

Dallas thumbed through his file and saw exactly what he'd expected to see. Webb labeled him a troublemaker and there were plenty of notes about the fights. But zero notes about Webb's beatings.

"We all had motive," Dallas mumbled. He tore his gaze from the folder and looked at her. "But did anyone other than us stand out?"

"Maybe." She opened her laptop and turned it on. "I used these notes and the timeline I created. As I said, you have a short window of opportunity. But some others didn't."

"Like Declan. He didn't do this." Dallas hoped not, anyway. "Besides, it might not have been one of the boys. Some of the girls had reason to hate Webb, too."

Joelle nodded. "Caitlyn Barnes. Remember, she and your brother Harlan were *together*."

Yeah, he remembered. Even though they were supervised, the teenage hormones had prevailed, and some of them had found ways to be *together*.

"You think Caitlyn could have killed Webb?" Dallas asked.

"Not really." Joelle huffed and sat down on the edge

of the desk. "And that's the problem. Webb wrote some negative things about her, even labeled her antisocial because she had all those piercings, crazy colored hair and wore black lipstick. But she wasn't a large girl. I can't see her overpowering a man like Webb. That's true for most of the residents, and the ones who were close to being physically his match either lack motive or opportunity."

"Doesn't take much *opportunity* to stab a drunk man," someone said.

Dallas automatically stood, reaching for his gun, and he spotted the man in the doorway. Rudy Simmons. The Rocky Creek caretaker.

"Didn't hear you come up," Dallas remarked. He didn't draw his gun, but he kept his hand poised over his holster and would keep it that way until he was sure the man wasn't a threat.

"Always been light on my feet," Rudy remarked. And apparently he still was because despite the fact he was wearing boots, he hardly made a sound as he strolled across the room toward them.

Dallas estimated the man was about fifty-five now but looked younger. There were threads of gray in his dark blond hair but few wrinkles. Everything about him was wiry and alert, and he definitely didn't put Dallas at ease.

"Marshal Walker." Rudy gave a dry smile and used his thumb to push back his battered cowboy hat that had probably once been white. It was a dingy tan color now. "You've come up in the world. From what I've heard, all of Kirby's boys have. Figure those badges will keep y'all out of jail?"

"Their innocence will do that," Joelle jumped to say before Dallas could speak. She stood, squared her shoulders and stared at Rudy. "And what's this about Webb being drunk? I interviewed you for hours, and you never mentioned that."

"Didn't I? Must have slipped my mind." His attention landed on the folders. "Find anything in those files?"

"If I did, it slipped my mind," Dallas drawled.

Rudy laughed, but the humor didn't make it to his eyes, and any trace of the laugh quickly faded. "I thought you were done with your *inquiry,*" he said to Joelle. "Figured you were on the verge of having somebody arrested."

"Not yet. In fact, I wanted to reinterview you and Sarah Webb."

That tightened Rudy's mouth. "You're not thinking I killed him?"

"Did you?" Dallas asked. He stood, slowly, but kept his gaze pinned to Rudy so he could see every bit of his response.

"I didn't." His jaw tightened even more. He pointed his finger first at Dallas and then at Joelle. "Nothing good can come from digging up all this old junk. In fact, it could be downright dangerous to your health."

Dallas moved out from behind the desk, putting himself in front of Joelle. "Is that some kind of threat?"

"No threat, *Marshal.* Just some sage advice. Of course, you were never good at taking advice, were you?"

"Not from you. And not from your old pal, Jonah Webb. Who killed him?" Dallas demanded.

Rudy got a cocky look on his face. "Rumor has it, you. Or your foster daddy."

"Rumors aren't worth a bucket of spit." Dallas was about to press for a real answer from Rudy, but the sound stopped him.

Footsteps.

A moment later, Sarah Webb appeared in the doorway. Good. They hadn't had to go to the cottage, after all.

Both of their suspects had come to them, and there was no doubt in Dallas's mind that both were indeed possible killers. There were very few adults who'd had access to Webb, but Rudy and she fit the bill.

"I saw you drive up," Sarah said, her voice soft. She gave both Joelle and Dallas a half smile, but she glared when her gaze landed on Rudy. "The truck with supplies just arrived. They need you to sign some papers."

Rudy returned the glare and extended it to Dallas and Joelle. "They're putting their noses in places they don't belong," he told Sarah.

"They're trying to find my husband's killer," she pointed out.

Sarah stepped inside the room, and Dallas got a better look at her. The years hadn't been as kind to her as they had Rudy. She was rail thin to the point of looking unhealthy, and the way she had her auburn hair pulled back from her face only made her features look more pointed and harsh. She'd never been an attractive woman and was less so now.

"They're trying to pin this on someone other than them," Rudy snapped back.

Sarah spared him another glance and went closer to the desk. As Rudy had done, she looked at the folders that Dallas and Joelle had been reading. She would have to be blind not to see the names on the files, and one of them was his own.

Sarah turned her gaze back to Dallas. "What Rudy isn't saying is that he and my husband were at odds when Jonah disappeared."

Joelle huffed and folded her arms over her chest. She zoomed right in on Rudy. "Yet something else that I'm just now hearing about. Why didn't you tell me this when I interviewed you?"

The man shrugged. "Didn't come to mind then. And besides, it wasn't important. Sarah here is just riled 'cause she couldn't find her witch's broom this morning."

Joelle opened her mouth to say something but thankfully backed off when Sarah whirled in Rudy's direction. They could probably learn a heck of lot more from Sarah and Rudy's argument than they could from the files.

"Insult me all you want, Rudy Simmons, but it doesn't change the truth, and the truth is my husband was on the verge of firing your sorry butt for stealing supplies meant for the kids."

"I didn't steal anything." Rudy didn't yell, but it was close. "Jonah just got confused, that's all. The inventory didn't add up, and he needed someone to blame other than his shoddy bookkeeping. Or maybe that was Sarah's shoddy bookkeeping. I figure she messed around with those numbers just to put a wedge between Jonah and me."

Sarah lifted her hands, palms up. "And why in sweet heaven would I do that?"

"Because Jonah and me was drinking buddies, weren't we?" Rudy readily answered.

They were. That was common knowledge, but this was the first Dallas had heard about issues with the bookkeeping. Judging from Joelle's reaction, she was just learning of it, as well.

"You seem to have forgotten some valuable bits of information during our chat," Joelle said to Rudy. "What else are you forgetting?"

"Don't take that tone with me." He rammed his thumb against his chest. "The only thing that's important here is that I didn't kill Jonah. In fact, if you're not willing to look in your own backyard—or bed—then look in Sarah's."

Dallas didn't care much for that bed reference, and

it took him a moment to get his teeth unclenched so he could speak. "What the hell does that mean?"

"Ain't it obvious?" Rudy countered. "Jonah was beating her over pretty good."

Sarah groaned softly. "My husband beat a lot of people." She looked at Dallas. "I'm sure you remember that."

"Yeah, I bet he does," Rudy volunteered. "The marshal was on the receiving end of Jonah's justice the very day he disappeared. A dispute over the scrawny kid if I remember rightly."

"Marshal Declan O'Malley," Joelle said. "And that dispute sent Declan to the infirmary for the night."

Where no one had actually seen him, according to Joelle. Still, it was clear from her tone that she didn't believe his kid brother was guilty. Or maybe she just didn't want Sarah and Rudy to believe it.

"Seems Jonah's whippings gave lots of people reason to kill him," Rudy added. "And none no more so than her." He tipped his head to Sarah, mumbled some profanity and walked out.

"What a despicable man," Sarah said after watching Rudy leave.

Dallas couldn't argue with that. "Why do you live so close to him? Why do you live here?" he amended. "This place can't hold many good memories for you."

"No, it doesn't. But it's home." She dodged his gaze. "And if I leave, then my son won't know where to find me."

"Billy," Joelle said. "I've been looking for him but so far, no luck."

"Because he doesn't want to be found." And that's all she said for several moments. When her gaze returned to look at Dallas, he saw her blinking back tears. "His father did some horrible things to Billy, and he's never forgiven me."

"He attempted suicide," Dallas said.

Sarah swallowed hard. Then nodded. "Sometimes, you just can't get over the bad things." Her attention shifted back to the folders. "Why did you come back? Have there been any breaks in the investigation?"

Joelle cleared her throat. "Someone found a knife that might have been used to kill your husband."

"Who found it?" Sarah asked.

"Sorry," Joelle answered. "I'd rather not say yet, but it was a hunting knife. Black wood handle with a curved tip for gutting animals."

Sarah's eyes widened. "Like Rudy's."

Dallas eyes widened, too. "Rudy has a knife like that?"

"Sure. He used to carry it with him all the time. Said it came in handy for skinning snakes."

Well, there'd been plenty of those around Rocky Creek, but maybe Rudy had used it to commit a murder. Of course, that didn't explain how Dallas's prints got on it. He didn't remember handling a knife like that, but it was possible he had. A lot had gone on in those few days leading up to Webb's disappearance.

"You'll question Rudy about the knife?" Sarah asked.

"Definitely," Dallas assured her.

She nodded, then gave a quick breath of relief. "I must be going. My quilting group will be arriving soon." She started to leave but then stopped. "Rudy was right about one thing, though. It might not be safe for you to continue this investigation. The person who killed my husband won't care for having his identity revealed."

Unlike Rudy's comments, Sarah's didn't sound like a threat, but there was still something uneasy about it. Or maybe it was the whole situation that made him uneasy.

"I worry about Kirby and all the ones he's took from here," Sarah went on. "That gives Kirby a powerful motive for murder."

Dallas had to shake his head. "How do you mean?"

"Well, Kirby was trying to close the place, but the day he disappeared, Jonah had gotten word that Rocky Creek was staying open."

That was news to Dallas. He looked at Joelle for verification, but she only shrugged. "Sarah told me that in the interview, but there's no proof."

Sarah made a sound of disagreement. "Maybe no written proof, but Jonah said he'd gotten the right people to back him up and that the place wouldn't be closed after all." She paused. "You should ask Kirby about this because Jonah told him, too. Kirby wasn't too pleased, of course. He wanted Rocky Creek shut down so it'd be easier to get custody of you boys."

Dallas wanted to know if this was something Joelle had discussed with Kirby, but he didn't intend to ask in front of Sarah.

"Guess I don't have to spell it out," Sarah went on, "that this could be Kirby's motive for killing Jonah."

"No, you don't have to spell it out," Dallas snapped. "Especially since there's no proof what your husband said was true."

Sarah didn't have much of a reaction to that, but she did check her watch. "I really must be going. Let me know if I can help you with anything." She turned and left.

He didn't say anything to Joelle until he heard Sarah's footsteps trail away, and even then Dallas went to the door and shut it.

He'd had his fill of surprise visitors for the day.

"Kirby didn't remember any conversation with Webb

about the facility staying open," Joelle said before he could ask.

So maybe Sarah was lying about the conversation and other things, too. Of course, he could say the same for Rudy.

"Interesting, huh?" Dallas said. "It sets off alarms in my head when someone volunteers that much info."

"Especially when they didn't volunteer it before." Joelle went to the window and looked out. "Maybe their tempers got the best of them, and they said more than they'd intended to say."

Maybe. Dallas joined her at the window and saw Rudy in the back unloading what appeared to be mulch and bags of soil from a truck. That explained why the grounds were still in such good shape—Rudy was actually doing his job.

But that didn't make him innocent.

"Do you remember Rudy ever carrying a knife?" Dallas asked her.

Joelle shook her head and turned toward him. Her arm accidentally brushed against his chest. A simple touch. But it cruised right through him.

"I'll ask Rudy about it," she said, glancing away. But not before he saw the discomfort, and maybe the heat, in her eyes.

He followed her gaze now past Rudy and to the heavily treed area on the west side of the grounds. He'd kissed her there, but then he'd kissed Joelle in a lot of different locations around Rocky Creek. This place was one gigantic memory. And it would have been easier if they'd all been bad.

But Dallas rethought that.

Loving Joelle had taught him plenty about just handing over his heart. If he hadn't learned that lesson from her, he would have had to learn it from someone else.

She swallowed hard. "I left you because I didn't have a choice," she said as if she'd known exactly what he was thinking.

Except her confession sounded like a little more than just a rehash of their past.

Something flashed through her eyes, as if she'd said too much, and her chin came up. "Besides, you never asked me to stay. You never told me if you even cared about me."

He was sure he looked at her as if she'd sprouted a third eye. "We were lovers," Dallas reminded her. "Frequent lovers," he added. "I figured that was proof enough I cared."

"No." She stretched that out a few syllables. "That was proof that you wanted to have sex with me."

Dallas huffed. "And that didn't tell you I cared?"

Apparently not, judging from the stony look she gave him. Dallas was about to press her on what he should have done and said back then—and how the devil this was somehow *his* fault—but Joelle moved, causing the sunlight to flash through the spot where she'd been.

At first Dallas wasn't sure he was seeing things, but he looked closer at the left-hand side of the window frame. The wood was stained a dark brown, but once he was close enough, Dallas saw the specks. A least a dozen tiny dots.

"What's wrong?" Joelle asked.

He ignored her for the time being and examined the other side. No specks there, and none on the sill. So, it wasn't part of the wood pattern, and it didn't look like the stain finish.

Joelle leaned in, examining it along with him. "What is that?"

"I'm thinking blood spatter."

She sucked in her breath. Looked closer. "You're right." Joelle grabbed her phone and used it to click several pictures. As soon as she was done with that, she made a call. "I need a CSI team out to the Rocky Creek Facility ASAP. Marshal Walker might have found something."

Dallas considered calling in someone from the marshals' staff, too, just so they'd have a second opinion, but he decided to wait and see what Joelle's CSI had to say. It might not even be blood spatter. But if it was...

"If it's Webb's blood, he could have been murdered here in this room," Joelle said, taking the words right out of his mouth.

"Or this could be from a beating Webb gave one of us."

"Yes." Her breath rose again. Her mouth tightened, and she was no doubt remembering the painful things that had gone on here.

He could tell she was fighting to hang on to her cool composure, and she stepped away from him. "I did a cursory check of the place when I first started the inquiry. I obviously missed that."

"Easy to miss," Dallas pointed out. "But if it turns out to be Webb's blood, the spatter and pattern might be able to tell us the height of the killer. Or more."

Her gaze shot back to his. "What do you mean?"

"Assailants who use knives often cut themselves during an attack. The killer's blood might be in that spatter." He looked around. "Or someplace nearby. Your CSI needs to go over the entire room."

She checked the time on her phone. Then looked at

the folders on the desk. "We should keep going through those while we're waiting."

Yeah. They should. But Joelle no longer looked too steady on her feet. Maybe the effects of the drugging. Maybe just the stress of seeing what might be a dead man's blood.

Dallas caught her arm and eased her into the chair behind the desk. He'd intended to move quickly away from her, but he found himself lingering.

She looked up at him and blinked. "Too many memories here." Her voice was a ragged whisper.

He managed a nod and hoped like hell she wasn't reliving the slap Webb had given her in this very office. Judging from the stark look on her face, though, she wasn't reliving the sexual stuff that'd gone on between them, either.

But he rethought that when he had a closer look at her eyes.

"I'm sorry," Joelle said a split second before she put her hand around the back of his neck and pulled him down to her.

Their mouths met. And, yeah, Dallas could have easily pulled away. *Easily.* But he didn't. He hauled Joelle up from the chair and kissed her the way he'd wanted to ever since he'd laid eyes on her at the church.

Everything suddenly turned frantic. Urgent. And hot, of course. There was always heat when it came to Joelle, and the taste of her jolted through him. Here were memories of a different kind. She tasted and felt right. Had the right fit in his arms. But he was no longer kissing a teenage girl.

And that made the situation even more dangerous.

Because Joelle knew how to kiss him right back.

Dallas pulled her closer to him, though she was already moving in that direction, and with just a shift of position, they were plastered against each other. He could feel every inch of her, and he had no doubt that she could feel every inch of him.

Like a trigger, his body got ready for sex. Old habits died hard, and even though he reminded himself that sex couldn't happen, he'd already crossed a big line just by carrying on with this kiss. And not stopping.

Thankfully, Joelle finally stopped. She jerked away from him, gasping for breath, and he saw the look. That look. The one she used to give him just seconds before he'd start pulling off her clothes.

"That probably helped, right?" she said. "I mean, it got it out of our systems."

Dallas didn't even attempt to agree with that whopper because the kiss was nothing but a reminder that getting Joelle out of his system was impossible. When kissing her, he'd forgotten all about the old wounds. And all about his vow of never forgiving the woman who'd abandoned him.

Hell, he'd forgotten how to think.

He was about to remind himself of how dangerous that was. Loss of focus and all that. But he stopped when Joelle froze. Her expression changed, and this time he was pretty sure it didn't have anything to do with wanting to have sex with him.

"Do you smell smoke?" she asked.

Dallas lifted his head. Yeah, he smelled it, all right. "Smoke," he spat out.

He hurried to the window, hoping that Rudy was burning some trash or something, but the man was no longer in sight. The bags of mulch and soil were piled on the ground, but there were no signs of a fire.

"Oh, God," he heard Joelle say.

Dallas whipped around in her direction, and he followed her gaze across the room.

Hell.

The smoke, black and thick, was seeping under the door.

Chapter Ten

Joelle's heart slammed against her chest.

"Sarah? Rudy?" she called out. She started across the room toward the door.

"No!" Dallas held her back. "Opening it could cause a back draft if there are flames on the other side."

He sounded so calm and sensible. And he was right, of course. Dallas definitely wasn't panicking the way Joelle felt that she was. She'd wanted to throw open the door and try to escape.

"Besides, if Sarah or Rudy was out there, they would have already called out to us," he reminded her.

True. Both had had plenty of time to leave the building and get out of hearing range.

"Move as far away from the door as possible," Dallas insisted. "And call 911 to get the fire department out here."

Joelle did as he'd asked while he made his way to the door. Toward the smoke that was getting thicker with each passing second. Dallas covered his mouth with one hand and pressed his other palm to the back of the scarred wood door.

"It's not hot so there's no fire nearby," he relayed to her.

Joelle had a split second of relief. Until Dallas tried to open the door. It didn't budge.

"It's locked," he said, cursing and coughing. He backed up a little and bashed his shoulder against the door not once but twice.

The lock held.

Of course it had.

Joelle had made sure it was secure because she hadn't wanted anyone breaking into the office and stealing or tampering with anything. But she was also sure of something else. There was no way either Dallas or she could have engaged that padlock while they were inside Webb's office.

Someone had locked them inside.

Mercy.

The panic soared through her again, and she tried to focus on how they could get out of there and find the person responsible. Hard to do, though. Because combined with the events of the day before, Joelle had to consider that this was another attempt to scare them.

Or kill them.

"Who had keys to the lock?" he asked.

"I'm not sure. I got mine from the governor's office." But it was something she'd find out as soon as possible.

Dallas looked up at the ceiling where there was a sprinkler head. "Not working?"

She shook her head. "I'm not sure. I didn't check them when I started the inquiry." But obviously it was out of commission. Either from not being used, or someone had tampered with it.

That didn't help steady her nerves. Did someone want to burn them alive?

"The window," Dallas said, hurrying back closer to her.

As they'd done before, they looked out the window

together. No Rudy. No fire escape or ladder, either. Just a one-story drop to the ground.

"This better not be locked, too," Dallas grumbled.

Her heart pounded even faster and harder, and Joelle held her breath while they tried to open the window.

It didn't budge.

But they kept trying, and finally it gave way. Thank God. Apparently, it was just temporarily jammed.

The smoke was still coming from the door, and it coiled right toward them, causing both Dallas and her to cough. He pushed her closer to the open window. To the fresh air. It helped, but in that position Joelle noticed the blood spatter again. That sent another slam of fear through her.

The smoke might destroy the evidence.

And maybe that's exactly what someone wanted. But how had the person known it was there? Dallas and she had just discovered it minutes earlier. Later, she'd need answers to that as well or decide if this was all just a horrible coincidence.

"We might have to jump," Dallas warned her.

He stuck his head out the window and looked around the grounds. Not an ordinary glance, but one of his cop-type surveillances.

Until then, it hadn't occurred to Joelle that someone might be out there, waiting to attack them. It might not be safe. But what choice did they have? If there was smoke, they had to assume there was also a fire that could eat through the entire building.

So they could burn or risk being shot.

"Stay close to the window," Dallas added. "Try not to take in too much smoke."

Joelle tried, but the smoke seemed to be coming in even faster and thicker. She yanked Dallas closer to the fresh air, too, when he started to cough harder. She wasn't sure how much longer they could stay in the room, but she was afraid the fire department wouldn't get there in time before they had to jump.

The drop suddenly seemed like a long way down.

Dallas and she could end up being hurt, and there was that possibility of someone being out there.

Even though her nerves were wired to the max, she couldn't get her mind off the blood spatter. "You think we can tear off that part of the window frame?" she asked.

Dallas looked at it, and then he made another check of the smoke and grounds. He grabbed the edges of the frame, obviously trying not to touch the spatter pattern, and he pulled hard. There wasn't room for Joelle to help, but she did keep watch out the window. That's how she spotted the movement.

And that movement came from Rudy.

He came running out from the side of the building. "I can't get in through the front door," Rudy yelled. "Somebody locked it up tight."

Great. Whoever was behind this had gone through a lot of trouble to trap them. Was that person Rudy? If so, they were looking down at the man who wanted them dead. Or at least the evidence destroyed.

"I'll get a ladder," Rudy added, and he raced back around the building and out of sight. Maybe he was genuinely trying to help them.

Or appear to be, anyway.

Dallas only glanced at the man, and he continued to pull and tug at the frame. "Hell. It's not budging." He looked at the ground again. "If we get down there in time, we might be able to use a hose to help keep the fire away from this room."

That was a long shot, but since she was coughing like

crazy, Joelle didn't see they had much of a choice. Of course, there was a chance that the smoke could damage the evidence, as well. She had the pictures on her phone, but she doubted the lab would be able to get much info from that. And certainly no DNA match.

It seemed to take an eternity for Rudy to return, but when he finally did, he had both a ladder and Sarah with him. The woman screamed and put her hand to her mouth when she saw the smoke.

"Start trying to put out the fire," Dallas instructed Rudy the moment the man had the ladder in place.

Rudy nodded and headed for the hose that was on the ground near some rosebushes. Sarah rushed toward them and held on to the ladder to anchor it in place. Both were obviously doing all the right things to save them, but Dallas clearly didn't trust either Sarah or Rudy. He drew his gun before he started down the ladder.

"Stay close to me," Dallas whispered to her.

Joelle did. She also grabbed her laptop and bag. There wasn't room for many of the folders, but she stuffed as many as she could into the bag.

"Hurry!" Dallas insisted.

She hooked the bag on her shoulder and climbed out the window as best she could. Not easy to do in heels and a skirt though. She moved down the rungs along with Dallas, and when he reached the ground, he lifted her the rest of the way down. He glanced at Sarah. Then Joelle.

"Come with me," he insisted, taking Joelle by the wrist.

Clearly, he wasn't going to leave her alone with Sarah, and that was fine with Joelle. Yes, she could probably overpower the woman if Sarah suddenly became unhinged and attacked, but Sarah was wearing a bulky sweater with pockets, and she could be concealing a weapon.

Or this could all be a massive overreaction on Joelle's part.

Still, someone had set fire to the place, and the most obvious culprits were the two people who were just a few feet away from them. Sarah was staring up at the smoke oozing through the window, seemingly frozen in shock. Rudy was pulling at the hose to get it to stretch closer to the building.

"Does your key work on the back door?" Dallas asked her.

"I think so." Her hands were trembling, and she was still coughing, but Joelle rifled through the bag, came up with the keys and handed them to Dallas.

As he'd done in Webb's office, he put his hand on the door. "Not hot," he relayed, and he proceeded to open the latch on the metal bar lock. While he did that, he looked back at Sarah. "Is there another hose?"

She gave a shaky nod. "On the side of the building. I'll get it."

Good. A second hose might be too little too late against a fire, but it was better than nothing.

Dallas threw open the door, and Joelle braced herself for the smoke to come billowing out. It didn't. There was some, but not nearly as much as there'd been in Webb's office.

"What the hell?" Dallas mumbled, and he stepped inside.

"Don't go in there." Joelle raced toward him and tried to pull him back. But she stopped when she looked around the back entry.

No fire.

Just wisps of smoke snaking along the floor.

The entry was a long opening, more like a corridor, with rooms feeding off it, and they could see all the way to the front door.

No fire there, either.

Dallas stepped in farther, and with his gun still drawn, he inched his way toward the stairs that were close to the entry.

"Keep watch behind us," he whispered.

Joelle looked behind them and spotted Rudy, who was pulling a hose into the entry. Joelle didn't see any sign of a weapon, thank God, but she kept watch just in case.

The smoke got much thicker as they approached the stairs, and Joelle started coughing again. Dallas moved her back, but not before she got a glimpse of the metal trashcan about halfway up the stairs.

Smoke was spewing from it.

"I'm betting there's another one just like it outside of Webb's office," Dallas mumbled, and he added some profanity.

It took a moment for that to sink in, and it didn't sink in well. There was perhaps no fire. Just someone playing a dangerous game.

After all, if they hadn't gotten the window open in Webb's office, they could have died from smoke inhalation.

Outside, Joelle heard the sounds of sirens. The fire department, no doubt. Even though there apparently was no actual blaze to put out, she still welcomed them because the smoke could damage the evidence inside the office. Plus, if Rudy or Sarah had done this, then it meant Dallas had some kind of backup with the firemen.

Dallas hurried her out of the building and into the backyard where Rudy was standing and shaking his head.

"Who the hell would do something like this?" Rudy snarled.

He sounded genuinely upset, but Joelle knew that sort of response could be faked. It was the same for Sarah. Dragging the hose around the side of the building, she appeared to be in near-panic mode.

But Joelle didn't trust either of them.

The sirens got louder, and she and Dallas hurried to the front where the driver brought the fire engine to a quick stop. The firemen jumped off.

"It appears to be just smoke," Dallas explained. He pulled back his jacket to show them his badge and pointed to the top floor. "But just in case it's more, try to keep the water damage to a minimum. There's evidence pertinent to a murder investigation in the locked room at the top of the stairs."

One of the firemen nodded, and they started pulling their gear from the truck. Hopefully, they'd be able to contain that smoke without damaging the blood spatter.

"Who did this?" she whispered to Dallas.

When he didn't answer, Joelle followed his gaze. Not to the building or the firemen. But to the woods on the right side of the grounds.

"Wait here with the firemen," Dallas insisted a split second before he took off running.

Joelle nearly went after him, but he shot her a stay-put glance and raced toward the thick cluster of trees.

She saw it then. Or rather she saw a man.

Definitely not Rudy. This guy was taller, bulkier, and he had on some kind of uniform, like those that the employees from the electric company wore. The moment that Dallas started toward him, the guy turned and ran.

Sweet heaven. What was going on now?

Joelle had been certain that either Rudy or Sarah had

set that smoke attack, but maybe she'd been wrong. Whoever this person was, running away wasn't a good sign.

She made another quick 911 call, and this time requested that the sheriff send someone out to Rocky Creek. The dispatcher said he would, but that it would take at least ten minutes.

That was too long.

A lot of things could go wrong in ten minutes.

Joelle desperately wanted to go closer, to see what was happening. And she especially wanted to help Dallas. But he'd be furious if she disobeyed his order to stay put. Besides, she could end up being a distraction and that could cause him to get hurt or worse.

"He needs help," she said to one of the firemen, but they were all focused on getting inside the building. One of them used bolt cutters to get through the lock, and they threw open the door.

Joelle couldn't stop herself. She went to the corner of the building so she could pick through the trees and see what was happening with Dallas. He had to be all right. And she didn't even try to push aside that she shouldn't be feeling this much for him. She'd deal with that later.

For now, she just wanted him safe.

She caught sight of the man in the uniform again. He was weaving through some trees, still running, and headed toward the back. Joelle knew just about every inch of the woods, and about a quarter of a mile away was the creek and plenty of trails that a person on foot could use to escape. She didn't know what part this man had played in locking them in, but she definitely wanted him caught.

Her heart was pounding again, right in her throat, and Joelle was about to beg the firemen to help Dallas. Then she saw him push aside a low-hanging limb just a few yards behind the man who was running away.

She grabbed on to one of the firemen and turned him in the direction of the chase. "Help him," she insisted.

When the fireman didn't move fast enough, Joelle forgot all about the sound reasoning she had for staying put. She started running toward Dallas and the man who was escaping.

Dallas launched himself forward, colliding with the man, and they fell to the ground where she could no longer see them. She hurried, tossing down her bag, so she could run even faster. Joelle bashed her way through the branches and had to skid to a stop so she didn't run into them.

Even though he was clearly outsized, Dallas dragged the man to his feet and held his gun beneath his chin.

"Talk," Dallas demanded. *"Now."*

Chapter Eleven

Dallas could do nothing more than watch and wait. Something he wasn't very good at doing.

Joelle must have felt the same because she was pacing the small observation room and had been doing that for the past hour, ever since Dallas's boss had insisted that's where they had to stay.

Because their presence could compromise the interrogation.

The problem was their suspect—aka the slimeball Dallas had chased down in the woods by Rocky Creek—wasn't saying anything so there was nothing to compromise. Every time Marshal Saul Warner had asked him a question, the man had mumbled that he wanted his attorney. Well, the attorney was on his way, but Dallas figured the lawyer would just tell him to keep up the silent treatment.

The same must have occurred to Joelle because her nerves were showing. It wasn't just the pacing. She was nibbling on her lip and looking many steps past the uneasy stage. With reason. She could have died today. Again. Dallas was used to facing danger, but this was probably eating away at her.

It also didn't help that Owen was just one interview room over from them. He was waiting for his lawyer as well to be questioned about the latest incident at Rocky Creek. Saul would do that interview, too, since he had specifically said he wanted Dallas and his brothers to stay away from the suspects.

"You okay?" Dallas asked her.

She didn't stop pacing or lip nibbling, but she did glance at him. "Who is he and why would he try to kill us?"

Those were million-dollar questions, but Dallas didn't have any good answers. He'd already suggested that someone had hired the moron to set the fire.

Or rather the smoke.

The fire was contained in the two metal trash cans where someone had placed ingredients that had essentially made smoke bombs. Crude but effective. The smoke could have indeed killed Joelle and him if they hadn't escaped through the window.

So was this some kind of warning for them to back off the investigation?

Maybe. And when this SOB started talking, that was one of the things Dallas wanted to know, right after he found out who'd hired this guy.

"Sarah and Rudy seemed mighty helpful," Dallas remarked. Not really answers to Joelle's questions, but it helped him to work out everything that was already whirling through his head. "A possible pretense, but we do have other suspects—Lindsey and Owen."

Joelle made a sound of agreement and then repeated it after several moments. Despite Rudy's and Sarah's opportunities to have set the smoke bombs and their somewhat lack of cooperation with the investigation, they still weren't Dallas's number one suspect.

Owen had that honor.

Dallas got up from the table where he'd been sitting

and went closer to Joelle. Probably a bad idea. With their nerves zinging, any closeness and touch could make things worse. Well, worse personally, anyway. But he was just sick and tired of seeing that troubled look on her face.

He pulled her into his arms.

She made another sound, this time of slight surprise. Yeah, he was surprised, too. After that mistake of a kiss in Webb's office, of all places, he'd vowed to keep his hands off Joelle.

By his calculations, that had lasted about three hours.

When it came to Joelle, his willpower just plain sucked.

Hers, too, apparently. Because she sure didn't budge from his arms. "It's no fun having people want us dead," she whispered. "I keep going over how to put an end to this, and other than Owen's arrest, I keep coming up blank."

Owen's arrest would do it. Well, it would if he was indeed behind these attacks, and if he was, then maybe Saul could squeeze out a confession during the interview.

Joelle eased back a little and looked him directly in the eyes. "I think I need to come clean."

Dallas had already considered that. Telling Saul about Owen's blackmail attempt, about everything. "If we're in jail, we can't clear our names," he reminded her.

She didn't respond to that, but she didn't take her gaze off him, either. Joelle pressed her hand to the side of his face, and she got that dreamy look. The one that let him know the attraction was still there.

"Damn you," she mumbled.

Dallas had anticipated she might say several things, but that wasn't one of them.

"I was over you," Joelle added, and her dreamy look morphed to narrowed eyes. "And then you do things like this to remind me why I hooked up with you in first place."

In case he hadn't understood, she dropped her eyes to the nonexistent space between them.

"Sorry," he said at the same moment that she said, "Dallas."

And she didn't say it with a mean tone. It was the tone to go along with the dreamy look she'd had just seconds earlier. A tone that was like the start of a kiss. Dallas might have obliged, too, if there hadn't been a sharp knock at the door. A split second later, it opened, and his brother Clayton leaned in.

Joelle and Dallas flew away from each other as if they'd been caught doing something wrong, but Clayton certainly hadn't missed it. Later, Dallas figured his brother would have questions about what was going on between them.

Yet something else Dallas couldn't answer.

"His lawyer's here." Clayton tipped his head to the adjoining interview room where their suspect and Saul were still engaged in a battle of silence.

A middle-aged guy in a suit walked in. He went straight to his client and started whispering something. There was an intercom system so that Dallas could hear normal conversation, but he definitely couldn't make out the whispers.

"We ran the suspect's prints," Clayton continued, "and the guy's name is Tim Avery, an on-and-off P.I. Mostly off. He sometimes works as a handyman, but there's no record of employment for the state and especially not Rocky Creek."

So there was no reason for the guy to have been there. Of course, Dallas had already guessed that since he'd tried to get away when Dallas had spotted him.

"Got back a couple of reports," Clayton continued. "Technically, I'm not supposed to see them, but they were hard to avoid since the fax machine is right by my desk. The first was Joelle's lab work."

That instantly got their attention, and both Joelle and Dallas turned toward Clayton.

"Someone slipped her a couple of prescription sleeping pills. Nothing serious. Not medically, anyway. I'm sure it wasn't fun for Joelle to be drugged."

"It wasn't." She wearily pushed her hair from her face. "Can we trace the prescription to Owen?"

"The local sheriff's working on that now," Clayton assured her.

Good, anything that would give them solid grounds to go after Owen.

"The other report is from the CSI team out at Rocky Creek," Clayton continued. "The smoke did damage the window frame some, but they're going to see what they can get. It's possible the DNA has degraded, though."

Joelle groaned softly. "Maybe they can at least get something from the spatter pattern."

"Maybe," Clayton agreed, but he didn't sound overly hopeful. "I thought you'd like to know that the Rocky Creek sheriff questioned both Rudy and Sarah. Both are claiming they had nothing to do with the fire."

That's exactly what Dallas figured they'd say. "Someone locked us in. And according to what Joelle found out about a half hour ago, neither of them should have had a key."

"I checked with the governor's office," Joelle added, "and the state official responsible for Rocky Creek had those bar locks installed to prevent anyone, including former employees, from going inside. There are only two keys. The state official has one in his possession, and I have the other."

"So someone had a key made," Clayton concluded. It wouldn't have been hard to do, but the person would have needed access. Of course, all their suspects probably had that, but maybe they could find a locksmith who would confirm which one had done it. Unless the lock had simply been manipulated with some kind of pick device.

Which was always a possibility.

"There's more," Clayton went on. "The CSIs found a bug in Webb's office, and I don't mean of the insect variety. There was a listening device mounted beneath the desk."

Dallas groaned. He went back through the things Joelle and he had discussed in that office. Like Sarah's revelation that the knife could be Rudy's. The blood spatter. Possible suspects. And yeah, even the old attraction.

Someone had overheard all of that.

But had that been the reason for the fire?

"My client is prepared to make a statement," the lawyer said, and it wasn't whispered so Dallas heard it loud and clear. It definitely got his attention.

Joelle's, too. She hurried closer to the observation glass.

"Mr. Avery is a private investigator and had nothing to do with setting the fire at the Rocky Creek facility," the lawyer insisted.

"Then why did he run?" Saul immediately fired back.

"Because his client hadn't wanted him to be seen."

"Client?" Dallas and Saul said in unison.

The lawyer nodded and said something that Dallas didn't catch. That's because at the same moment he heard the footsteps in the hall, and someone spoke. It was a voice he recognized.

Lindsey Downing.

Clayton moved inside the observation room so they could see Lindsey. She motioned toward the lawyer, and much to Dallas's surprise, the man stepped out of the interview and spoke to her in the hall. Again, a whispered conversation.

One that gave Dallas a bad feeling.

Joelle looked at Dallas, silently questioning what was going on, but he had to shake his head.

"I hired Tim Avery," Lindsey said when the lawyer finally stepped away and returned to where Avery was waiting. She looked directly at Joelle. "I wanted him to follow you."

Joelle's mouth dropped open. "Why?"

And while Dallas wanted to ask the woman a whole lot more, that question was a good start. So was turning off the audio on the intercom. He didn't want to compromise the interview by having Avery's lawyer claim that his client's rights had been violated in any way.

"I hired him to get proof that you were sleeping with Dallas," Lindsey readily admitted.

Dallas was sure that Joelle looked as stunned as he felt. "But I'm not," Joelle argued.

Lindsey dismissed that with a wave of her hand. "A matter of time. I know all about the history you've had with Dallas, and I figured once you two became lovers again that I wanted proof to show Owen."

Dallas repeated Joelle's "Why?"

"So he'd break things off with her, of course." Lindsey's tone indicated that the reason was obvious.

But it wasn't obvious to Dallas. Nor to Joelle, judging by the way she groaned. Before either of them could respond, Clayton's phone rang, and he stepped outside the room to take the call.

"What did Owen tell you about our so-called engagement?" Joelle demanded from Lindsey.

"We've got another visitor," Clayton called out. "Must be our lucky day," he added, his voice dripping with sarcasm.

More footsteps, and someone cleared their throat. A moment later, Owen appeared in the doorway. Obviously, he'd heard their voices from the interview room where he was supposed to have been waiting, and he looked about as pleased with Lindsey's accusations and revelations as Joelle did.

"I told Lindsey the truth." Owen planted his stare on Joelle. "And the truth is we're in love and are getting married."

The words were right, with even a touch of affection in them, but Dallas knew it was a coldhearted threat for Joelle to play along with the lie.

"But she doesn't love you," Lindsey snapped. "I can see it, and you could, too, if you'd just look at her. She's still in love with the marshal."

"I'm not." But then Joelle shook her head. "And it doesn't have any bearing on what's happening." She turned her own stare on Owen. "Someone tried to kill us again. Any idea who might have done that?"

Owen glanced at Lindsey. "I heard her say that she hired the man to follow you. Maybe she hired him to set the fire, too."

Lindsey made a helpless sound, part gasp, part sob, and she snapped toward Owen. "I love you, but I couldn't do something like that." Tears sprang to her eyes. "I just wanted you to see what she is, and that she's not the right woman for you."

Owen's expression softened a little, and he brushed

his hand down Lindsey's arm. "Yes, she is, and you're just going to have to accept that."

Lindsey made a sound of outrage, and it was so loud that it had Saul stepping from the interview room. He took a look at them all, cursed and eased the door shut.

"This better not be a witness interrogation," Saul warned.

"It's not," Dallas quickly assured him. "Owen didn't stay in the interview room, and she showed up out of the blue." He pointed to Lindsey. "She claims she hired the man inside that room to watch Joelle." And then he pointed to Owen. "I'm guessing he's just here to tell more lies."

Owen smiled, probably because he thought Dallas couldn't elaborate on those lies.

Especially the lies that mattered.

"Uh, guys," Clayton said, stepping back into the mix. "I got some news." He looked first at Dallas and then motioned for Saul to step aside.

Saul did, but he didn't just back away from them, he went much farther down the hall with Clayton. All of them watched and tried to listen, but Dallas couldn't hear a thing. Whatever Clayton said to him caused Saul's eyes to widen, and Dallas could have sworn the man blew out a short breath of relief.

"You're sure?" Saul pressed.

"The fax is on the way," Clayton explained.

"What's going on?" Joelle whispered to him.

Dallas had to shake his head. He had no idea, but they didn't have to wait long because both Saul and Clayton started back toward them.

"You," Saul said, pointing to Lindsey. He hitched his thumb to one of the interview rooms. "Wait there. No reason for you to be in on this conversation."

Lindsey huffed and looked around as if she might argue, but she didn't. Maybe because she figured out it was an argument she couldn't win. She stormed away, went inside the room and slammed the door.

"The lab just sent us the preliminary test results on the knife and handkerchief," Saul announced to the rest of them. "The knife's clean. No prints. No DNA."

Dallas had to do a mental double take. "What?"

"Nothing on it," Saul verified. "That puts you and your brothers in the clear. Not Kirby though."

Any relief that Dallas felt went flying out the window. "What the hell does that mean?"

"The handkerchief had Kirby's DNA and some blood spots that the lab hasn't been able to ID yet. If it's Webb's blood…" But Saul didn't finish that thought.

Didn't have to.

Kirby would be questioned, maybe even charged with the murder, if it was Webb's blood.

Except Dallas wasn't going to let that happen.

"You're sure the knife was clean?" Joelle pressed. And Dallas knew why. After all, she'd had a knife tested with his prints and Webb's blood. Now, this knife was clean.

Dallas looked at Owen, waiting for the man to say something, but Owen only gave him one of those smug smiles that made Dallas want to mop the barn floor with him.

"The person who sent me that knife is playing some kind of game," Owen said, his attention fastened to Joelle and Dallas. "Makes me think he or she might have something else tucked away. Something that will prove who killed Webb."

Ah, there it was. The carefully veiled threat. Owen had the real knife with Dallas's prints, and he'd be more than willing to hand it over if Joelle didn't go through with the wedding.

"A game?" Dallas repeated. He glared at Owen. "Why would this *person* give the marshals a fake?"

Owen lifted his shoulder. "Maybe the person likes to see you squirm?"

Yeah, Owen would like that, and he was dancing them around like puppets.

Dallas looked at Joelle, and a dozen things passed between them. They didn't say a word to each other, but he could see in her eyes and body language that it was time to put and an end to this. Well, an end to part of it, anyway.

Owen's lies.

"I'll start," she said in a whisper to Dallas, and she turned to Saul. "During the course of my interviews into Webb's death, I ran across certain testimony that implicates Owen in various white-collar crimes."

"Wait a minute!" Owen jumped between Joelle and Saul, or rather he tried, but Dallas yanked him back and put him against the wall.

"If you do this, you'll regret it," Owen mumbled so that only Dallas could hear. "Joelle, too."

Maybe. But at this point, it was better than playing games with the likes of Owen.

"You'd better sit down, Saul," Dallas warned his boss. "Because when this is done, you'll need to arrest me."

"And me," Joelle volunteered. She yanked off her engagement ring and slapped it into Owen's hand.

Saul cursed a blue streak and dropped down into the chair. "Tell me," he ordered.

Chapter Twelve

Joelle felt as if she'd just weathered a fierce storm. But there was another one headed her way.

Maybe several, she amended, when Dallas ushered her inside the ranch house.

Judging from his body language and tone, his latest phone conversation wasn't going well. Joelle had already had enough bad news for the day without adding more, but it appeared that's what she was going to get.

"How'd that happen?" Dallas snapped.

Joelle knew the caller was Clayton—she'd seen his name on Dallas's cell phone screen—which meant this likely had something to do with the investigation.

Maybe Saul Warner had decided to arrest Dallas and her, after all. When the senior marshal had ordered them away from headquarters earlier, he'd said he had to evaluate all the evidence and testimonies before he could make a decision about filing charges.

Saul had taken Dallas's badge, though.

That hadn't exactly been a surprise, but Joelle knew that Dallas was upset about it. Since he was thirteen, he'd wanted to be a marshal, and now that might be taken away from him permanently.

Of course, her job was a goner, too. Saul hadn't called the governor, but eventually he'd have to do it, and that meant Joelle had to bite the bullet and call her boss first. During that conversation, she would have to tender her resignation and wait to see if she was facing jail time.

As bad as that was—and it was *bad*—it still paled in comparison to the fact that someone had tried to kill Dallas and her. Hard to hunt for a new job with a killer breathing down their backs. That meant they had to find Webb's killer. Or whoever was after them.

Maybe that was the same person.

Maybe not.

After all, Lindsey had hired the P.I. to *follow* her, so maybe the woman was responsible for the attacks. Still, it was an overkill approach to stop her marriage to Owen. And if that had been Lindsey's plan, then she no longer had a reason to wish Joelle dead since the wedding was definitely off.

That was the one good thing to come out of this.

She wouldn't have to pretend to be engaged to Owen any longer.

Dallas stayed in the entry, finishing his call, but Joelle was so exhausted that she headed for the guest room where she'd slept the night before. When she stepped into the hall, she saw a nurse come out of Kirby's room. The woman put her finger to her mouth in a stay-quiet gesture and closed Kirby's door.

Later, Kirby would be another issue they'd have to handle. There was no way Dallas would let the man go to jail, and besides, he was too fragile for that anyway. That wouldn't stop them from putting him under house arrest though, and Joelle made a mental note to contact a friend who specialized in criminal law. Dallas, Kirby and she might need someone like that before this was all over.

She dropped down onto the foot of the bed, kicked off

the heels that were killing her feet and was contemplating what to do first—shower, eat, sleep.

Or cry.

There were so many emotions whirling inside her. Old memories that suddenly didn't feel so old because of the kiss in Webb's office. She couldn't even berate herself for it or swear that it wouldn't happen again because one of the big moments of a day filled with big moments was that she knew she wasn't over Dallas.

Never had been.

And wishing things were different wasn't going to make her feelings go away. Besides, Joelle wasn't even sure she wanted things to be different. Not her feelings, anyway.

Speaking of the devil, she heard movement in the hall, lifted her head and spotted Dallas in the doorway. He'd obviously finished his phone call, and with his attention fastened to her, he propped his shoulder against the jamb. He stared at her but didn't come closer.

"Feel up to coming into the kitchen?" he asked, his voice low. He tipped his head toward Kirby's door. "Don't want to wake him. And besides, you need to eat."

She did. Her stomach was growling, and she agreed with the part about not waking Kirby. Still, it took a little effort for her to get off the bed. Joelle didn't bother with her shoes. Barefoot, she just followed Dallas to the kitchen.

"What's wrong?" she asked. She didn't think his expression was solely from the fatigue and the ordeal they'd just gone through.

He didn't answer her right away. Dallas pulled out a glass dish of leftover spaghetti and meatballs and put it in the microwave. "Owen will be out of jail soon. His lawyer is already working on posting his bail."

Joelle glanced at the time on the stove clock, groaned and sank down on one of the stools at the breakfast bar. "He spent only a few hours in a holding cell."

Dallas lifted his shoulder. "He can afford good lawyers. And obviously bail. Besides, the charges weren't as serious as they should have been. Only obstruction of justice and making a false statement about the fake knife that he turned over to the marshals."

No attempted murder charge, but then it would have been hard to pin that on him. For now. However, Joelle could maybe get those white-collar crimes she'd uncovered to stick.

"What about the real knife, the one with your prints?" she asked.

"Owen has agreed to turn it over and claims he was only holding it back because he was afraid it would implicate you."

What a snake. He was holding it back to blackmail them. "You'll tell your boss the truth?"

Dallas nodded. "When the results are back. I'd like to delay the charges brought against us."

Yes, and there would be charges. Joelle didn't see a way around that.

"What about Kirby?" She hated to bring it up, but it was his DNA they'd found on the handkerchief, and the marshals would have to deal with that.

She silently cursed Owen for adding this stress to a man who could be on his deathbed.

"Saul's going to wait on the handkerchief, too," Dallas explained. His breath and expression were weary. "But after all the test results are in on the real knife, Saul will have no choice but to question Kirby. And maybe file charges," he added in a mumble.

Yes. That meant they only had a couple of days at most

to try to find the real killer. It might not get Dallas, Kirby and her out of hot water, but delivering a killer to the marshals would end the threats against them and maybe stop Kirby and Dallas from being arrested for murder.

And that brought her to another concern.

"Once the governor finds out that there'll be charges brought against me, I seriously doubt he'll give me permission to continue this investigation."

Dallas looked back at her, the corner of his mouth lifting into a weary smile. "Guess you'll have to go rogue like me. Because I'm not stopping until I clear Kirby's name."

"And your own." When Dallas turned around, her gaze fell to his rodeo belt where his badge should have been. "I'm sorry."

"Couldn't be helped." He said it offhanded enough, but she saw the hurt in his eyes.

Dallas took the dish from the microwave, put in on the counter between them and grabbed some forks. "I say let's skip the plates."

As hungry as she was, Joelle thought that was a great idea, but when he passed her one of the forks, his hand brushed against hers. With everything else going on, the last thing that should cross her mind was his touch.

But it did anyway.

Dallas didn't ease back, either. He stood there, his index finger covering hers. "I'm thinking this is a bad idea," he drawled.

"A terrible one," she confirmed.

Of course, that didn't stop her from leaning forward. Dallas leaned in, too. His mouth brushed against hers. It barely qualified as a kiss, but because it was Dallas's mouth, it slammed through her. Not all pleasant, either, since the brush-kiss only made her ache for him.

"We always were good at this," he mumbled, and the movement caused more touching of his lips against hers.

"Too good. You taught me how to kiss," Joelle reminded him.

"Must be why you're so good at it," he joked.

Dallas chuckled. More movement. More touching. More barely qualifying kisses that were still making her burn. Despite the burn, despite everything, it felt good to be with him like this. And even better than good, it felt right.

It wasn't.

But Joelle was suddenly having a hard time remembering why it was wrong.

He slid his hand around her neck, and while keeping it in place, Dallas came around the breakfast counter and eased her off the seat.

Right into his arms.

He didn't kiss her though. With his forehead bunched up, he just looked down at her as if trying to decide what to do.

"You're not going to say no, are you?" His forehead bunching up even more.

"No to what?" she asked.

"Anything that happens between us in the next few minutes," he clarified.

Oh.

That.

Joelle shook her head. "There won't be any *nos* from me in the next few minutes."

Maybe not ever when it came to Dallas. And she wasn't exactly proud that Dallas was her hormonal Achilles' heel. It wasn't hard to understand why. He stood there, all cowboy, in his jeans and boots. He'd left his Stetson in the entry, but that only allowed her to see his rumpled, bedroom hair.

Bedroom eyes, too.

Ironic, since they'd never actually had sex in a bedroom. Every time they'd been together at the ranch, they'd had to sneak away so that Webb or someone else wouldn't see them.

Dallas cursed, squeezed his eyes shut, and she thought he might indeed back away. But he didn't. His eyes opened, he dragged her to him and kissed her the way her body was begging for him to kiss her.

It was like stepping back in time. But better, too. They weren't the same people they'd been back then, and Dallas somehow brought all of that and their shared past right into that kiss. Joelle heard herself make a helpless sound of surrender, and she was lost. *Willingly.*

Dallas brought her closer to him until they were wrapped in each other's arms. Until everything was hot and spinning out of control. The spinning got worse when he kissed her neck.

And lower.

He pushed aside the gold heart necklace and kissed her throat.

Then lower.

To the tops of her breasts, which he kissed through her clothes.

She'd known that nothing could stay simple with them. A kiss couldn't just be a kiss. And when he deepened it and slid his hand between them to touch her breasts, Joelle figured they were only minutes away from hauling each other off to bed.

She fought to remember why that wasn't a good idea, but the buzzing sound cut through her thoughts. Through the heat.

Dallas cursed, pulled back and yanked the phone from his pocket. "What now?" he snarled.

Joelle glanced at the screen, expecting to see a message from one of his brothers or maybe his boss. There was a lot going on with the investigation, and there'd hopefully be updates. Good ones. She'd had her fill of bad news for a lifetime.

But the message was from Owen.

They groaned in unison. "What does he want now?" Joelle asked.

Dallas held up the screen for her to have a better look. "Here's something you should know," the message said.

Joelle felt her heart thud against her chest, and it wasn't a residual effect of the kiss. She shouldn't have such a reaction to anything Owen might say, but her mind immediately went in a bad direction.

But then she shook her head.

Owen didn't know about *that*.

"It's probably another threat to get you to marry him," Dallas mumbled, and he clicked on the attachment that Owen had sent with the message.

It seemed to take an eternity for the page to load, and it wasn't a photograph as Joelle had originally thought. She wouldn't have put it past Owen to show them more so-called evidence that would send them to jail.

But it was a document of some kind.

"What the hell?" Dallas said, and he positioned his phone closer so he could have a better look.

Joelle went to his side so she could do that same thing, and when she saw the wording at the top of the document, all the air vanished from her lungs. She staggered back, and in the same motion, she caught onto Dallas's wrist. Trying to stop him from reading it.

Oh, God.

It was too late.

Dallas's gaze slashed to hers, his eyes already narrowed while he shook his head. Everything about him was demanding an explanation.

"It's a birth certificate," he said.

She had no choice but to nod. Joelle tried to speak, tried to explain, but her throat clamped shut.

Dallas had trouble speaking, too. The shock and maybe the outrage had turned his jaw to iron. He got right in her face. "You have a baby?"

Chapter Thirteen

Dallas felt as if someone had punched him.

He wanted Joelle to look at the document on his phone and shout out a firm denial that she had a child. He wanted her to say it was another of Owen's tricks. A lie meant to tear them apart so he could get some measure of revenge for his failed attempt to get Joelle to marry him.

But Joelle didn't deny anything.

She just stood there, shaking her head, while every drop of color drained from her face.

Hell.

It was true.

Joelle had a baby.

Cursing, Dallas forced himself to look at the document again, and his attention zipped over the lines. It was a birth certificate, all right.

Amber Reese Tate.

Joelle was listed as the mother. The info on the father had been left blank, but Reese was Dallas's middle name. Then he quickly did the math. The baby had been born fifteen and a half years ago.

Seven months after Joelle had left Rocky Creek.

And him.

"She's my baby," Dallas heard himself mumble. But not a baby. A teenager.

Joelle was still shaking her head, and tears spilled down her cheeks. Normally, those tears would have sent him reaching for her. So he could comfort her. But he didn't want to comfort her now. He wanted to wring her neck.

"You kept my child from me," he said.

"I didn't," she said, her voice hoarse and raw.

He showed her the document again and dared her to repeat that lie.

"I didn't keep her from you," Joelle repeated.

She yanked something from her blouse. The heart-shaped locket, and she opened it. On the left side of the heart was a baby's picture. His picture was on the right, exactly where he'd put it sixteen years ago when he'd given it to her.

So it was the same locket.

Before he'd seen that birth certificate, Dallas might have asked her why she still wore it after all these years, but there was only one thing he wanted to know now.

"Where is she?" he demanded, pointing to the picture.

Joelle's breath rattled in her throat. "She died."

Nothing could have prepared him for that.

Nothing.

Dallas stumbled back and probably would have fallen to his knees if he hadn't caught on to the counter.

"Amber was born nearly two months early," Joelle continued, speaking in a whisper. "She only lived a few hours."

The tears were coming faster now, streaking down her face, but Dallas still couldn't go to her. The pain was almost unbearable. He'd fathered a child. A child he'd never seen, never known about. And he couldn't do either of those things, ever.

Because his child had died.

Dallas had so many questions firing through his head. Why hadn't Joelle told him? And why the hell had he learned about this from Owen? How had Owen gotten his filthy hands on the birth certificate? Dallas had wanted answers to all of that—but dealing with Joelle was first on the list.

"The doctors did everything they could to save her," Joelle went on. She blindly fumbled behind her, located the chair and sat back down. "But she was just too weak." Her voice broke. "She was buried on my eighteenth birthday."

Dallas could practically see the images of that. Joelle, no more than a kid herself, burying a child. *Their* child. It must have broken her heart, the way it was doing to him now, but Dallas still couldn't go to her.

Not with this anger and hurt stabbing through him.

"You should have told me you were carrying my child," he finally managed to say. His teeth were clenched. Every muscle in his body was so stiff he was in physical pain.

"I considered it," Joelle said. "But I also considered what you would have done if I'd told you."

"I would have married you!" he practically shouted.

"Exactly. You would have married me and tossed away your scholarship. You wouldn't have become a marshal."

"You don't know that. I would have found a way to do both, but you didn't even give me a chance."

She paused, gathered her breath. "I was going to tell you. I saw her face after she was born, and I decided that you should know. But she never even opened her eyes, Dallas."

Hell. Each word was like a knife to the heart.

"I should have been there," he insisted.

"I thought I was protecting you," Joelle insisted right back. He jabbed his index finger at her. "You weren't. You were keeping a secret that wasn't yours to keep. I fathered her, and I should have had the chance to see her."

The pain crushed him, hard, and it mixed with another surge of anger that was stronger than the first. Dallas wasn't sure how to deal with it, but he knew he didn't want any interruptions. Unfortunately, he heard the movement in the hall and snapped toward the visitor, figuring it was Kirby's nurse, Jackie Hall. It was, but she wasn't alone.

Kirby was with her.

He was leaning against the nurse, but he was on the verge of falling so Dallas rushed to him. "You shouldn't be out of bed."

"Had to," Kirby mumbled. "Heard you arguing."

"I'm sorry," Joelle said, going to him. "It's all right."

"No, it's not." Kirby dragged in a ragged breath. "I knew about the baby, but I didn't tell you, either."

Dallas swung his gaze back to her, but Joelle shook her head. "You knew?" she asked Kirby.

"Highly suspected," he confirmed. "And I didn't do a thing to encourage you to tell Dallas."

Damn. How could these two people—who supposedly cared about him—do something like this?

How?

Dallas was sure they didn't have the right answer because it wasn't right, plain and simple.

"I went to visit Joelle," Kirby said, his voice getting weaker with each word. "To check on her and make sure things were going okay with her foster family. But they were in the backyard when I got there, and before they spotted me I overheard them talking about a baby."

Joelle made a sound as if trying to recall that. "You heard me say I was pregnant?"

"Not exactly, but I put one and one together. I also did

some other math. You were seventeen, and Dallas was a year older. An adult in the eyes of the law."

Her breath became thin. "But Dallas and I had been lovers for months, well before he turned eighteen. And the baby was probably conceived when we were both underage."

"Yeah," Kirby conceded. "I'm not saying it was right, but you were a ward of the state then, and I didn't want anyone trying to make an example out of Dallas by filing charges against him."

"Oh, mercy," she mumbled. Dallas wanted to mumble something much harsher.

"I was wrong not to tell you what I suspected," Kirby added, looking at Dallas now. "So if you've got to blame somebody, son, blame me."

He didn't want to blame anyone. He wanted back the opportunity he should have been given sixteen years ago.

Kirby groaned, a sound deep within his throat, and he would have collapsed if all three of them hadn't caught him. His father had once outweighed Dallas by a good thirty pounds, but the cancer had eaten away at him, making it easy for Dallas to scoop him up in his arms.

"You got to forgive Joelle," Kirby mumbled. "And me. I made a lot of mistakes raising you boys, and I told myself it's because I wanted you to grow up right."

Yeah. Dallas had always known that was one of Kirby's concerns. He owed Kirby, but Dallas couldn't give the forgiveness that he'd just requested. Not now, anyway.

"We'll talk about this later," Dallas settled for saying. He put Kirby back into bed, covered him with the quilt and turned to the nurse. "Make sure he stays put."

The woman gave a shaky nod, and though she probably didn't know what was going on, she had to realize it was serious.

And it was.

Dallas marched back into the hall, grabbed Joelle and headed not back toward the kitchen but outside to the front porch where they could hopefully finish this conversation without Kirby hearing.

"I'm not blaming him for this," Dallas insisted. But part of him was doing just that.

She swiped at the tears but more came. "Kirby has his reasons for not telling you, and I had mine. I didn't think of the age difference between us back then, but Kirby was right about someone maybe using it to arrest you. The main reason I didn't tell you was because I was worried you wouldn't go through with college."

"I wouldn't have," Dallas snapped. "But that was a decision for me and me alone to make." He couldn't help it, Dallas cursed again. "Hell, no wonder you wouldn't see me or answer my calls. You didn't want me to know I was about to be a father."

That was one thing explained. He'd never been able to figure out how Joelle could go from red-hot to ice-cold in such a short period of time, but yeah, a pregnancy would do it. Part of him hurt to the core that she'd had to go through that alone. At seventeen, no less. But another part of him just hurt.

"You need time," Joelle murmured.

"I'm not sure that'll help." But it was the pain talking. He did need time. He had to sort all of this out and come to terms with what he'd lost.

And what he had lost was his baby.

The lump in his throat was so thick he wasn't sure he could breathe. It felt as if someone had a fist clamped around his heart.

God, he hadn't expected anything to hurt this much.

His phone buzzed again, and he nearly bashed it on the

porch, but then he saw it wasn't Owen and his trouble-making attempts this time. Nor was it a message.

It was a call from Clayton.

The last thing Dallas wanted to do was talk to anyone, but he knew in his gut that his brother wouldn't have called if it weren't important. And with all the irons they had in the fire, it was a call he had to take.

"Yeah?" Dallas answered, unable to hold back the anger and other emotion in his voice.

"Uh," Clayton said. "You okay?"

Dallas ignored that question and went with one of his own. "Why'd you call?"

"I thought you'd want to know that I'm out at Rocky Creek."

That was the last place one of them should be right now. "What are you doing there? What went wrong?"

"Nothing's wrong. I'm actually calling with some good news. From the sound of things, you could use it right about now."

"Yeah," Dallas said. He glanced at Joelle. She was pacing now. And still crying. Hell's bells. What a tangled mess this was.

"I've been here for about a half hour," Clayton continued. "Quietly observing the CSI team. Not with Saul's permission or knowledge, but I called in a few favors. Don't worry. I'm not in the actual building. Figured I wouldn't want to call into question anything they might find." He paused. "They found some things, Dallas."

Even though he doubted Joelle could have heard what Clayton said, she must have sensed something because she stopped pacing and moved closer. Dallas wasn't feeling very generous, but he put the call on speaker so she could hear.

"The initial tests indicate that it's Webb's blood on the

window frame. Better yet, it's a cast-off pattern consistent with someone who plunged the knife into Webb and then drew it back to stab him again."

"Any way to use the pattern to determine the killer?" Joelle asked.

"They're working on it," Clayton answered. "Not just the blood on the frame, but there are spatters on the wall invisible to the naked eye that the luminol lit up. They might be able to get some details about where the attack started. And who started it."

Good. Luminol was a chemical spray that could detect even small amounts of blood. Too bad Dallas's mind was still in a horrible place right now because this conversation was important.

"From what I heard from my contact inside," Clayton went on, "there was some indication of blood on the floor, too."

Joelle shook her head. "Why wasn't this detected sixteen years ago?"

"Because it wasn't tested, that's why. Webb was just a missing person, and the local sheriff then checked for any signs of foul play, but he missed the spatter on the frame."

Easy to miss. The sunlight had been just right for Joelle to see it and then point it out to him.

"Without the luminol, you can't see the blood on the floor, either," his brother continued. "Plus, it looks as if someone tried to clean it up. There are swipes and smears. The CSIs might be able to determine if Webb was dragged from his office after he was stabbed and how his body was taken from the building. And that could give us more clues about the killer."

"Yeah," Dallas agreed.

"I know what you're thinking. This new evidence could point to Kirby, but I don't believe it will. Kirby's well over six feet tall, and from the CSIs' initial observations, they're thinking the killer was someone shorter."

Someone shorter would still implicate a lot of people. Including Declan and Joelle. But it would also point the finger at Sarah, Rudy and a dozen other kids who were living there at the time.

"I haven't gotten to the best part of what they found," Clayton went on. "When they were looking at the blood on the floor, they found a loose board, and one of them lifted it. There was a makeshift safe."

Now that grabbed his attention. "What's in it?"

"Don't know yet. It's locked, and it's too heavy and big to lift out of the floor. Plus, they want to make sure it's not booby trapped."

Good point. Webb would have done something like that, but what was so important that he would want to seal it off in a secret safe?

Clayton huffed. "What the hell's the matter with you? This is good news, Dallas. Or it could be, anyway. This is the first break we've had in the investigation."

"I know. I, uh, just have, well, something else going on."

"Not a good time for that," Clayton countered. "I'll call you back as soon as I hear anything else."

Dallas mumbled a thanks, ended the call and tried to get to a place in his head where he could deal with the news about his daughter and everything else. He looked at Joelle, who was clearly waiting for him to say something.

Maybe that he could forgive her.

But Dallas wasn't anywhere near that just yet. He groaned and turned to go back inside. However, he made it only a step before his phone buzzed.

"Owen," he grumbled when he saw the name on the screen.

"I'll talk to him," Joelle insisted, and her teary voice was replaced with a huge amount of anger. Anger she'd no doubt aim at the man who'd sent that birth certificate.

Dallas was furious with Owen, too, but he had to accept that if Owen hadn't delivered the bombshell, then he might have never learned about his and Joelle's child.

He didn't give the phone to Joelle even though she was motioning for it. Dallas pressed the button to take the call, and like Clayton's, he put it on speaker.

"Did you like my little present, Joelle?" Owen immediately asked.

"You bastard." She moved closer to the phone. "You've done a lot of slimy low-life things in your life, but this takes the prize. How did you know? How did you find out?"

"You can thank Lindsey for it," Owen happily volunteered. "She hired a P.I. to dig into your past. Looking for dirt, I'd imagine, so she could use it to break us up. Little did she know she'd find this."

And *this* was tearing at Dallas's heart.

Yes, Joelle should have told him. Kirby, too. But he wasn't pleased that Owen had used something like his baby's birth certificate as a way to get back at Joelle.

"If I were you, I'd watch your back," Dallas said to Owen. "Lindsey's unhinged, if you ask me, and now that Joelle's called off the wedding, Lindsey will probably think that's her invitation to go after you. How far do you think she'll go when you reject her?"

Owen didn't respond to that. Yeah, it was a small victory, but Dallas was glad to get in that dig. Besides, he really believed that Lindsey could be dangerous, and with Joelle out of the picture, maybe she'd aim some of her efforts and venom at Owen.

"Stay out of my life," Dallas warned the man, and he jabbed the button to end the call.

He'd barely had time to put his phone in his pocket when it buzzed yet again. No profanity this time. He was too tired and too aggravated to curse, but if it was Owen, Dallas intended to find him and beat some sense into him.

But it was Clayton again.

"I hope this is good news," Dallas said when he took the call.

"Sorry." And with just that one word, Dallas heard the concern in his brother's voice.

"What's wrong?" Joelle asked before Dallas could.

"We've got a problem. A big one. You need to get out here to Rocky Creek. *Fast.*"

Chapter Fourteen

Joelle tried to focus on the phone conversation that Dallas was having with Clayton. It was his third call since the one on the porch back at the ranch. They'd left immediately after that, but Dallas had stayed in contact with Clayton, who was on the scene at Rocky Creek.

Where heaven knows what was happening.

Joelle still wasn't sure what was going on, and Dallas still seemed to be gathering all the details. That's why this call was no doubt important, but Dallas hadn't put this one on speaker, so she could only hear his side of the conversation.

Which wasn't telling her much.

Of course, she was partly to blame since she was having zero luck concentrating on anything other than what Dallas had learned about their baby.

Even now, all these years later, the pain felt fresh and raw. Like a huge wound that would never heal. She'd tried to bury that pain with work, but she hadn't managed to do that. It was always there, just below the surface.

Now it was right on top again.

Dallas had said often he wasn't the forgive-and-forget type. He wasn't. And this was much more than he'd ever had to face.

He would never forgive her.

That broke what little of her heart wasn't already broken. Sixteen years ago she'd resigned herself to the fact that she could never have Dallas, but it hurt to know that he would hate her for the rest of his life.

Dallas ended the call, and Joelle waited for news of why Clayton had insisted they come out to Rocky Creek. He didn't volunteer anything, and his jaw muscles were set in iron again. Joelle wasn't sure if that was because of the baby news or what Clayton had told him. Either way, it wasn't going to be a pleasant evening.

"What's going on at Rocky Creek?" she finally asked.

Dallas took his time answering and pulled in a weary breath. "In addition to the secret floor safe, the CSIs found blood on the wooden banister. They decided to photograph it and then remove pieces of it so they could swab underneath. Rudy burst in and told them to stop, that he wouldn't let them destroy the place."

"Oh, mercy." Joelle added a groan.

"It gets worse. Rudy pulled a gun on the CSIs and ordered them out of the building. Now he's holed up in there, threatening to burn the place down if he doesn't talk to me."

She shook her head. "Why you?"

"Who knows. He won't say. Won't talk to Clayton, either. He just keeps pointing the gun and demanding to talk to me."

Joelle tried to come up with a logical reason for that demand, but she couldn't think of one.

Unless Rudy thought that the evidence would incriminate him.

"Maybe the standoff is a ruse so Rudy can destroy any evidence that might be in the secret safe," Joelle offered. "And he's adding to that ruse by demanding to see you."

Dallas paused as if considering that. "The safe is still

locked. The CSIs couldn't get it open, and there's no indication that it's been opened or tampered with in years. Besides, Clayton has Rudy in his sights."

Since she'd read the background reports on all of Dallas's foster brothers, she knew that Clayton had sniper training. "Clayton's armed with a rifle?"

"Yeah. And if necessary, he'll take Rudy out."

Oh, God. Not another death. Joelle wasn't especially fond of Rudy, but he was a human being and besides, he might be able to clear up who killed Webb.

Rudy might even confess to doing the deed himself.

That would solve some of their problems and would stop Dallas or Kirby from going to jail. Not her, though. She would still have to face charges of suppressing information about the knife. But a confession would be a huge start.

And then maybe Dallas and she could deal with everything else.

"I'm sorry," Joelle whispered.

At first she wasn't sure Dallas had even heard her, but when he tossed her a glance, she realized he had. Joelle figured that meant he wasn't ready to talk about it. Maybe never would be. But she had to try.

"I'm trying to make myself remember that you were a kid yourself," he said before she could say anything else.

Joelle held her breath. Waiting. But he didn't say anything else for several long moments.

"I can't put all of this on you," Dallas added.

No. This was not where she wanted this guilt trip to go. "And I don't want you to put it on Kirby, either. He loved you and wanted the best for you. Plus my new foster parents were telling me the same thing I was thinking—that if you knew about the pregnancy, it would ruin your life."

"But they didn't seem to mind that it'd ruin yours.

Did they happen to mention that when they were advising you?"

The pain cut even deeper. It was so hard going back to that time and place. All those memories. Some precious. Some horrible. She'd been ill equipped to deal with everything she was feeling and had managed to push some of it deep inside.

It was all coming back. And Joelle had to wonder how she could cope with it all over again.

"My foster parents wanted me to put the baby up for adoption," she said when she could gather her breath. "I, uh, said no, and eventually they agreed that I could stay with them, and they'd help me raise the baby." That required another pause. "Then, of course, Amber didn't make it."

More silence. His jaw muscles stirred, and he kept his focus straight ahead when he turned onto Rocky Creek Road.

"I'm sorry for everything you went through, but you should have told me," Dallas finally said, and his inflection let her know that he'd just closed the subject.

No forgiveness.

Not for her. And not for Kirby.

She hated that she'd put this wedge between them, but once this case was finished and she was out of Dallas's life, Joelle figured Kirby could mend things. If the cancer didn't take him first, that is.

Ahead, she saw the Rocky Creek facility, and even though the sun was setting, there was just enough light left for her to see the people milling around. Some CSIs in their uniforms. A couple of locals, too. Clayton was there, literally on top of a truck, and he had a rifle pointed at the building.

"Hell," Dallas mumbled.

Like her, he probably didn't want to deal with anything that involved rifles and standoffs, but apparently they had no choice.

When Dallas's truck got closer, she saw the makeshift roadblock that had been set up with traffic cones. Sarah was standing next to one of the cones, her attention on whatever was happening inside.

Dallas stopped the truck, and they both got out.

"Rudy's gone crazy," Sarah informed them immediately. "He's locked himself inside and won't come out."

Dallas looked past her at the man who was walking up the road from the building. He made a beeline for them.

"I'm Sheriff Bruce Shelton," the lanky man greeted. He took a badge from his pocket, flashed it. He looked more cowboy than cop with his jeans, boots and Stetson, and he was wearing a gun in an old-fashioned hip holster.

"Dallas Walker," he greeted back, and Joelle noted that he hadn't included his title of marshal. Probably because he no longer had a badge. "And this is Joelle Tate from the governor's office."

"This way." The sheriff motioned for them to follow him. When Sarah started to go with them, he shook his head. "Alrcady told you to stay put. If you don't, you'll be the one facing charges."

"But Rudy's threatening to burn down the building," Sarah protested. "I can't let him do that. The place is part of my home. He has no right to even be inside."

"We'll deal with him," Sheriff Shelton answered, and he kept walking.

Thankfully, Sarah stayed put, but she did continue to call out for them to stop Rudy.

"We have phone contact with Rudy," the sheriff explained to them. "And your brother volunteered to cover the shot if it came down to it."

Cover the shot. A sterile term for sniper duty. Of course, from everything she remembered about him, Clayton had a level head, and he wouldn't shoot Rudy unless there was no other choice.

"Has Rudy destroyed any evidence?" Joelle asked.

"Not that we can tell. So far he's stayed right in the entry near the stairs."

Well, that was something at least, but it didn't mean Rudy wouldn't follow through on his threat to burn the place down.

When they approached the truck where Clayton was positioned, one of the men, a deputy, handed the sheriff a cell phone.

"Rudy, Marshal Walker just arrived," the sheriff explained. "Miss Tate, too. Now say your peace to them like you said you wanted, and then let's end this."

"Dallas?" Rudy immediately said.

"I'm here." Dallas moved closer to the phone. "Why'd you call me out here?"

"Because this is a setup." Rudy's words were slurred. "And I'm not going to jail for something I didn't do."

Dallas glanced around, probably to see if anyone knew what Rudy meant by that, but the sheriff, deputies and others just shook their heads.

"Rudy, what the hell are you talking about?" Dallas demanded.

"The so-called evidence these city boys are finding. Webb's blood," he clarified in a mocking tone. "Well, it was planted there, I tell you, and it was planted to set me up."

Great. The man had either lost it or had been misinformed.

"The CSIs are collecting evidence, Rudy," Dallas assured him. "They weren't there to frame you. We only want to know the truth about what happened to Webb."

"The truth?" he howled. Joelle looked inside and saw that Rudy was pacing. Clearly agitated. And maybe even drunk because he wasn't too steady on his feet. "You want the truth, you should be asking Sarah a thing or two."

"I heard that!" Sarah shouted. "Don't listen to that drunk fool. He's lied so much he doesn't know how to tell the truth anymore."

"Sarah's the one who told me this was a setup," Rudy continued as if he hadn't heard her, and he probably hadn't. Sarah wasn't yards away from the cell phone that was on speaker. "She's a resourceful woman, and she knows how to set up a man like me to take the blame for something she did."

"What do you mean by resourceful?" Dallas pressed Rudy.

Rudy cursed, shook his head and stumbled again. "I mean she coulda created them spots of blood on the window to make it look like I killed her husband."

"Did you kill him?" Joelle came right out and asked.

"No." Rudy made a groaning sound. "Jonah was my friend. And if you're looking for a killer, look at Sarah."

Dallas huffed. "How could Sarah have gotten Webb's blood to plant anywhere to set you up? The guy's been dead for sixteen years."

"She probably saved the cleaning rags she used to wipe up his blood. Saved them and then used them today so these city boys would find it."

"Listen to yourself," Dallas continued. "One minute you say that Sarah warned you this was a setup, and now you're saying she's the one who tampered with evidence."

"Because that's what she said!" Rudy stopped, cursed some more and held on to the wall, probably to stop himself from falling. "She did this. She riled me up. Confused me."

"Or maybe you misunderstood," Joelle offered. She glanced back at Sarah, and for just a split second, she thought the woman had a smug look. But maybe it was the twilight playing tricks on her eyes.

"Didn't misunderstand her," Rudy snarled. "Who do you think really ran this place all these years? Not Jonah, that's for sure. Nothing went on around here without Sarah knowing about it. And there wasn't one kid who took a beatin' without Sarah making sure it happened."

That sent an uneasy feeling through Joelle. She'd never liked Sarah, had always thought of her as a shadow of a woman. Had she been wrong? Of course, even if Sarah had pressed for the abuse, it'd still been Webb who'd carried it out.

"It's like what went on with that knife," Rudy continued, yanking Joelle's attention back to him.

"What knife?" Dallas asked. He met Joelle's gaze, and she could see the concern in his eyes.

"My knife. The one I always used for skinnin' snakes. She took it when I was out doing some yard work. Took it from my truck, and she brought it to Jonah and fibbed. Said she found it on Declan."

This was the first Joelle was hearing about any of this, and there was no mention of it in any of the notes she read, but Dallas made a slight sound as if recalling something. "Webb brought Declan and me into his office one afternoon and showed us the knife." He looked at Joelle. "I forgot all about that until now."

"That's right. He showed you, and you picked it up. Looked at it real good and said you'd never seen it before. Declan didn't touch it but he said the same. Jonah told me all about it. Then, he said Sarah took the knife and put it away somewhere."

Oh, God. Had that really happened? Or was this the ranting of a drunk man who might be trying to cover his own guilt? After all, the knife very well might have been Rudy's.

"Rudy's making it sound like I did something wrong," Sarah shouted. "I didn't steal the knife from his truck. I found it in the boys' bathroom and took the knife to Jonah. After he showed it to some of the boys, I put it in Jonah's desk drawer just like he told me to do. I told Jonah it might be Rudy's, and he said he'd ask him about it later."

The sheriff motioned for Sarah to stay quiet. "Keep talking," he instructed Rudy.

"Jonah didn't know the knife was mine," Rudy went on. "When he described it and I told him it was, he looked for it but said Sarah must have taken it. I think Sarah used that knife to kill Jonah, and if she did, Marshal, she'll try to pin his killin' on me or you. Me because it was my knife and you because your prints were on it."

Dallas's gaze met Joelle's, and she saw the questions in his eyes. Of course, Rudy's accusations didn't address their number-one suspect.

"Did Owen have access to that knife?" Joelle asked.

"Owen?" she heard Rudy question, and he shook his head. "I doubt it. Well, unless Sarah gave it to him."

"I didn't," she called out. "I put in the drawer, and I don't know why it wasn't there when Jonah looked for it."

Maybe because someone had taken it.

Someone like Owen.

Of course, Sarah could have taken it, too.

Dallas looked back at her as if thinking the same thing.

"I swear to you," he said to the woman, "that I'll get to the bottom of this. I won't stop until I find the killer."

If he'd meant it as a warning, it worked. In fact, it sounded more like a guaranteed threat. It certainly hushed Rudy and had Sarah looking a little uncomfortable.

"This knife isn't important," Sarah responded after several moments. "All this stuff Rudy is spouting about happened months before Jonah was killed," Sarah added. "It doesn't make sense that I'd hide a knife all that time."

It would if Sarah intended to keep it for protection against an abusive man. But that didn't rule out someone else doing the same thing.

Joelle wanted to ask Sarah if Owen or anyone else had access to that drawer. Of course, if Owen had taken it, that meant he'd kept it hidden away after all these years. That was a long time to withhold evidence.

Unless he used it to murder Webb.

If Owen had known about Dallas's prints being on the knife, then he could have kept it simply to pin the blame on Dallas. But then that meant whoever the real killer was had used gloves so that only Dallas's prints would be there.

Could Owen have thought to take those kind of precautions when he was only seventeen years old?

Maybe.

And if he had, it meant Webb's murder hadn't happened in the heat of the moment. It was premeditated.

Yes, she definitely had to ask Sarah some questions, including ones about that safe. Had she even known about it? And did she have any idea what was inside it?

Joelle turned to do just that, but she only made it a few steps toward Sarah before Dallas and the sheriff cursed. She whirled back around and saw that Rudy was no longer in the entry. He'd dropped his gun and was running up the stairs.

"Don't shoot him," the sheriff called out to Clayton. "He's not armed."

But that didn't meant he wasn't dangerous. "Webb's office," Joelle said on a rise of breath. "He might try to set it on fire."

Dallas, Clayton and the others started running. "Make sure the back of the building is secured," Dallas shouted, and Clayton headed that way.

Joelle ran after them, cursing her heels, which were only slowing her down. Dallas made it to the front of the building first, and with his gun drawn, he threw open the door and raced toward the stairs. She saw Rudy's gun on the floor where he'd discarded it, but she prayed he didn't have another weapon on him. Joelle didn't want this to turn into a shootout with Dallas caught in the middle.

The sheriff retrieved Rudy's gun, stuck it in his pocket and barreled up the stairs behind Dallas. "Wait here," he insisted.

Joelle didn't want to wait. She wanted to stop Rudy from hurting Dallas and destroying evidence, but since she wasn't armed and probably wouldn't be able to restrain Rudy, she did as the sheriff said and stayed put.

The seconds crawled, and she looked around to see if Sarah had followed them, but the woman was nowhere in sight. Later, Joelle would need to find her and ask her about Owen's possible access to the knife.

"Rudy went down the laundry chute," she heard Dallas shout.

Joelle remembered exactly where that was, and it wasn't anywhere near Webb's office. Maybe Rudy hadn't planned to set it on fire after all, but she didn't breathe easier yet because Dallas was still up there, and Rudy was clearly trying to escape.

And that's when she remembered that the chute emptied into the basement. Basements were a rarity in Texas, but Rocky Creek had one that was used as a laundry and storage area.

She also remembered something else.

"There are basement access doors on the ends of the building," she called out to the Dallas and the others who were upstairs. She immediately heard someone headed back down the hall toward the stairs.

Joelle hurried to the front door and looked out. Still no sign of Sarah, but it didn't take long for her to spot some movement.

Rudy.

He must have cut the lock on the east side of the building because he staggered out into the near darkness and headed toward the thick woods that led to the creek. And his trailer.

"Rudy's getting away!" she yelled, and it didn't take long for Dallas to appear on the stairs.

He practically jumped down the steps and raced outside. "Which way did he go?"

Joelle pointed in the direction where she'd last seen him just as the sound cracked through the air. Her heart dropped. Because she knew that sound.

A gunshot.

Oh, God. Was someone shooting at them?

She couldn't tell if the bullet had hit anything, but it had seemed to her that it'd been fired close by. Of course, miles was too close as far as she was concerned.

"Get inside," Dallas ordered.

Joelle stepped back into the entry, but Dallas didn't do the same. Using the building for cover, he went outside. So did the sheriff, and one of the deputies leaned out from the door and fanned a bright flashlight into the woods. She didn't see Rudy, but the deputy and others inched closer toward the trees.

Joelle peeked out, praying that there wouldn't be another shot and that no one was hurt. But that thought had no sooner crossed her mind when she heard someone shout.

Rudy.

"I've been hit," he yelled. "Someone's trying to kill me."

That put her heart in her throat. She wasn't fond of the man, but she didn't want him dead.

But someone did.

Who?

And why?

Joelle glanced around, looking for Sarah. Or God forbid, even Owen, but she didn't see anyone, only Dallas and other law enforcement.

The deputy's flashlight slashed over the dark woods, and he came to an abrupt stop when the light caught the movement. All of the lawmen aimed their weapons in the direction.

"Stop!" Dallas called out. "And put your hands in the air."

Joelle held her breath, hoping that Rudy would do just that so the standoff would end. But then she heard Dallas curse.

"What the hell?" he mumbled.

Joelle leaned out even farther so she could see what had prompted that response and the puzzled mumblings of the other lawmen. Thanks to the spray of light, she saw that the person in the woods had indeed done as Dallas had ordered.

But it wasn't Rudy.

It was a woman.

With her hands lifted in the air, the woman turned toward them. Joelle couldn't see if she was armed, but she did get a good look at the woman's face.

Lindsey.

What the devil was she doing at Rocky Creek, and why had she shot Rudy?

Chapter Fifteen

Dallas hadn't figured this night could get any longer or more frustrating, but he was obviously wrong. The latest phone call had proven that, and he hung up wondering if he was ever going to catch a break on this investigation.

Joelle's huff let him know she felt the same way.

"I can tell from your expression that it's bad news," she mumbled.

Well, it wasn't the news he'd wanted. Before Dallas explained, he opened the door to the ranch house and motioned for her to keep her voice down. It was late, nearly midnight, and he didn't want to wake up Kirby.

And Kirby was another subject he needed to tackle.

Take a number.

Dallas wasn't pleased with his foster father withholding the pregnancy news, but a heart-to-heart with Kirby would have to wait. There were actually more pressing things.

Like Lindsey.

Dallas tugged off his Stetson and hooked it on the peg. He also set the security system. "The sheriff tested Lindsey for gunshot residue," he told a waiting Joelle. "And they didn't find a gun on her or anywhere else in the woods."

Joelle's mouth dropped open for a moment. "But she was there, and someone shot Rudy."

Both of those things were one hundred percent true. Rudy had indeed been shot. Well, sort of. A bullet had grazed his arm, but it wasn't serious. He'd only needed a few stitches. However, none of the evidence was pointing to Lindsey as the woman who'd shot him.

If anyone had.

"Clayton said Rudy's wound was superficial," Dallas added in a whisper.

She stared at him a moment, processing that, and then groaned. "Are you saying Rudy could have shot himself?" But she waved him off before he could confirm that. "He could have done it to throw suspicion off himself, so that we wouldn't believe he killed Webb."

Bingo.

And the problem was, it was working. Yes, Rudy had been arrested for the standoff at the building, but he hadn't fired at any police officers and hadn't damaged any property that anyone could find. Coupled with the fact that he had no police record of any kind, and Dallas figured Rudy would be out of jail by morning.

Maybe earlier.

"The sheriff gave Rudy a Breathalyzer, and he was way over the legal limit," Dallas continued. "I'm sure his lawyer will say that was the reason for his erratic behavior."

Another soft groan, and she leaned her back against the door. "And what's Lindsey's lawyer saying?"

"She hasn't asked for one, and the truth is, she might not need to. Unless they find a gun in those woods with her prints, the most the sheriff can charge her with is trespassing."

And it was doubtful he'd even charge her with that

since there weren't any no-trespassing signs posted in that area of the woods.

She closed her eyes a moment, opened them and met his gaze. "Well, at least all the evidence is still intact."

Yeah, but they both knew that evidence might produce nothing that they didn't already have. It was Webb's blood on the window frame and possibly the stairs, and the CSIs might even be able to guess at the height of the killer. But that wouldn't give them a name.

But whatever was in that safe might.

"I did convince the sheriff to remove all the documents from Webb's office," Dallas explained to her. "The safe and its contents, too. They'll be moved to the marshals' office for now, but I didn't want anyone destroying something that could catch a killer."

She made a weary sound of agreement. "I'm betting Sarah and Rudy won't like you taking those things."

That was a correct bet. According to the sheriff, both had pitched hissy fits. They were too damn territorial for Dallas's liking, especially since their insane need to preserve Rocky Creek could also be preserving the identity of the killer.

"I need a drink." In fact, he needed several of them, but Dallas would settle for one and then crash because he figured tomorrow wouldn't be any easier than today. "And I need to toss this." It was the rest of their fast food dinner that they'd grabbed on the drive back to the ranch.

Joelle pushed herself away from the door and followed him into the kitchen where he dropped the bag in the trash. Judging from the exhaustion on her face, he'd expected her to say good-night and head for the guest room, but instead she motioned for him to hand her a beer when he took one from the fridge.

She twisted off the top, had a sip and made a face.

Maybe beer wasn't her usual drink, but she still had another sip of it. "Look, I know this isn't something you want to hear, but I'm going to say it anyway."

Hell. Dallas knew where this conversation was going, and he wanted no part of it. "Not now," he warned. But he might as well have been talking to the air.

"I did what I thought was right at the time," Joelle continued. And she didn't just continue. When he started to walk out, she grabbed his arm. "You can be mad at me all you want, but you're going to hear me say I'm sorry for keeping the pregnancy a secret."

Dallas could have easily thrown off her hand and put off this conversation for another decade or so, but he didn't. Maybe it was the fatigue, the beer or the pain in Joelle's eyes, but he nodded.

"Apology accepted," he said.

She blinked. "You mean that?"

"Yeah."

She got closer, studying his eyes. Then, she frowned. "You're just saying that to get me off your back."

"That's part of it," he readily admitted. "The other part is I do forgive you. I do understand."

She still looked skeptical.

"Now, I need to know just one thing. How did you get past this?" He tapped his chest, his heart. "Because even though I didn't know my baby existed before today, it's killing me to know we lost her."

"Yes." And the tears instantly sprang to her eyes.

Dallas hadn't wanted to make Joelle cry again, but the pain and tears were all part of this.

Joelle shook her head, then swiped at the tears. "Time helps. Some," she amended. More tears came. And she tapped the locket she wore around her neck. "It helps that I have her picture with me everywhere I go. I can make you a copy. And give you copies of some other photos that my foster mother took during those few hours that Amber was alive."

Dallas managed a nod. "I'd like that."

They stood there staring at each other, and when Joelle's tears didn't stop, Dallas took her beer and put it aside. Put his on the counter, too, and he hooked his arm around her waist to lead her toward the guest room. She didn't put up a fight.

"You need to sleep," he insisted.

She didn't put up a fight about that, either. In fact, it was pretty clear that Joelle wasn't going to protest anything he did tonight.

And that made this a very dangerous situation.

The attraction was always there between them. Maybe even stronger than it'd been when they were teenagers. It would be so easy to start with a kiss that would land them both in the bed for some hot, satisfying sex.

But she wasn't in any shape for that.

They were both dealing with the hurt from the loss of their baby. Both were battling the adrenaline crash from the hellish day. Plenty of good reasons for him to back away, but Dallas still had a hard time doing it.

The next sound he heard sure didn't help.

It was the low rumble of thunder outside. He hadn't had time to check the weather, but from the sound of it, there was a storm moving in. Joelle wasn't a fan of bad weather. In fact, years ago it'd been something close to a phobia.

She froze in the doorway of the guest room, her attention zooming right to the window where the rain was already tapping against the glass. He felt her muscles go stiff, and her breathing became a little uneven.

"I can sleep outside your room," he offered. Not exactly the offer he would have made when they were at Rocky Creek. In those days, he'd risked Webb's wrath by sneaking into her room and holding her until she fell asleep.

No fear of Webb's wrath tonight, but holding her—like kissing—would lead to sex.

He cursed.

Hell, anything at this point might lead to it.

She looked up at him. Her eyes were wide. "It'll be okay."

That was a lie, but to call her on it meant he'd have to make that hold-her offer that would get them on the bed together. He would do it. If she pressed it.

Dallas waited for her to press it.

And he cursed himself again because part of him wanted her to press.

Joelle was breathing through her mouth now, and her warm breath was hitting his neck. Almost like a kiss.

Like before, she studied his eyes. Maybe trying to figure out what to do. But he studied her eyes, too, and he saw the heat there. One touch. Just a brush of his body against hers, and both of them would be goners.

"Yes," she whispered because she no doubt knew exactly what he was thinking. She also knew why he hadn't already latched on to her and started what would be stupid to start.

Just when Dallas was sure his willpower had turned to dust, she shook her head and stepped away. "It'll be okay," Joelle repeated.

She grimaced at the next rumble of thunder, but while grimacing, she stepped away from him. "Good night, Dallas," she whispered. "Get some sleep."

There was zero chance of that. He was aroused beyond belief, and that aroused part of him was begging him to go to her.

He didn't.

Dallas used every bit of willpower and forced himself to step back and shut the door between them. The last thing he saw was the disappointment, and the heat, flash through Joelle's eyes.

Cursing himself, cursing her, and cursing anything and everything he could think of, he went to his room, stripped down to his boxers and got ready for bed.

Alone.

Unlike it was for Joelle, the rain soothed him, and he might have been able to fall asleep if it weren't for the blasted thoughts that just wouldn't leave him alone. He tossed, turned and groaned when a bolt of lightning jagged through the sky and flashed through his room. The thunder followed, more than a few rumblings this time, and the rain came down harder.

No way was Joelle sleeping through this.

That only caused the ache to return, but he reminded himself that she was a grown woman, not the teenager who'd been terrified of storms. It didn't help with the thoughts or the ache, but thankfully the next jolt of lightning was farther away. Ditto for the thunder.

Dallas watched the minutes tick off on the clock next to his bed. And soon, there was no more lightning. No more thunder. Just the gentle rain that was barely making a sound.

Now Joelle would sleep.

And he hoped the same for him.

He forced his eyes shut but had to reopen them immediately when he heard a sound. Footsteps. Since he knew from the phone calls he'd made that none of his brothers was home, he thought maybe it was Kirby's nurse.

Or worse, Kirby.

He threw back the covers just as someone threw open his door.

Definitely not Kirby.

Joelle.

Since there were night-lights on in the hall, he had no trouble spotting her. She was wearing a barely there red nightshirt that didn't cover much.

"Don't say a word," she ordered in a whisper.

She didn't have to worry about him speaking. His mouth had gone bone dry, and that got much worse when she closed the door, locked it and pulled off the nightshirt over her head. She dropped it on the floor.

Instantly she was naked, and he got an instant erection.

"And please don't think about turning me down," Joelle added.

Dallas had plenty of thoughts, but that wasn't one of them. And even if he had, turning her down would have pretty much been impossible when she slid like a siren into his bed. He didn't even let her head hit the pillow. He hauled her closer and put his mouth to hers.

And she kissed him right back.

It didn't start off gentle, and Dallas figured he stood zero chance of trying to slow things down. Maybe because they'd been all these years without each other. That caused an uneasy feeling inside him. A fleeting one because Joelle moved her body against him, lining up her sex with his, and the feeling of raw need overtook any uneasiness.

She didn't just stop there, either. She started with touching. Her hand on his chest, and then it made her way to his stomach.

And, no doubt, she would then head lower.

Just the thought of it had him seeing stars and had

his erection urging him to take her at breakneck speed. Breakneck was fine sometimes, but he wanted this to last a little longer than Joelle apparently had in mind.

That's when Dallas made some adjustments of his own. He shifted, dragging her beneath him and pinned her hands to the bed. He kissed her. First her mouth. And then her neck. Because he knew every inch of her body, he also knew what would make her burn. A long, slow kiss at the base of her throat.

So that's what he gave her.

Joelle made a sharp moan but then clamped her teeth over her bottom lip to muffle the sound. But she darn sure didn't muffle her movements. She lifted her hips, the heels of her feet sinking into the mattress, and all that hot, wet heat between her legs brushed against him.

Oh, yeah. He saw stars, all right.

And Joelle started with the touching and kissing again. Dallas held her back. Well, as much as he could, and he kissed her neck. Her breasts and her stomach. He would have done more sampling, but she caught his hair and yanked him back up.

"We'll do that later," she promised.

Hell. The woman knew how to make him crazy and keep him that way.

Since it was obvious that he couldn't keep the pace slow, Dallas fumbled in the nightstand drawer, located a condom and put it on. Joelle helped, and either she was very bad at putting on a condom or else she wanted to torture him. By the time she finally got the darn thing in place, he was well past being ready.

She thrust her hips forward just as he entered her, and Dallas had to muffle his own sharp groan. This one was from pure pleasure. The sensation of being inside her shot through him. Like lightning. And probably just as hot because he lost his breath and didn't care if he ever got it back.

He moved.

Joelle did, too.

The pace and rhythm was fast and hard and only got faster and harder. With one hand he grabbed her bottom so he could control this war they'd waged on each other. With his other hand, he caught her hair and bent her head so that he could go after her neck.

Yeah, it was playing dirty.

But she was so caught up in the pleasure of it that she slowed down just enough for Dallas to take her the way he wanted to take her. A few strokes of slow and easy that had her making that little purring whimper that had haunted him for all these years.

Joelle purred, all right. And with another of those siren moves, she lifted herself to him one last time.

Before she shattered.

"Dallas," she said, her voice strained.

That was enough for him. All he needed. He gathered her close and let Joelle finish what she'd started.

Chapter Sixteen

Joelle felt the unfamiliar warmth next to her body, and her eyes flew open. She would have scrambled right off the bed if someone hadn't grabbed her and pulled her back.

Dallas was that warmth.

And the memories of what had caused it came flooding back. She was at the ranch. In his bed. And she'd brazenly thrown herself at him.

Thank goodness he hadn't refused her.

Well, she hoped it was thank goodness. There would probably be consequences, but Joelle pushed those aside, turned and looked up at the man who had her wrapped in his arms.

"It's around five," he grumbled, though she had no idea how he knew that since he didn't even open his eyes to check the time.

She glanced at the clock. Yep, he was right. Barely five in the morning. The sun wasn't even up yet. And although they had a ton of stuff to do and discuss, she settled back against him and let herself enjoy the moment.

"I've never woken up next to you before," she whispered. Joelle glanced down at their positions on the bed. "You hog the covers."

He chuckled, the sound a low rumble in his chest, and he pulled her even closer against him. More warmth.

More memories, too. The memories got a little fresher when he nuzzled the back of her neck.

She made a shameless sound of pleasure. "You've gotten better at this over the years. All that practice you did on me must have helped."

"You weren't practice, Joelle." His voice was still a sleepy mumble so it took her a moment to realize what he'd said.

And what he didn't say.

"Then what was I?" she asked.

"Trouble." Dallas rolled her over and kissed her. "You still are."

It seemed like a light answer for something she knew they'd soon have to discuss. Or rather clarify. After all, never once had he told her how he felt about her. But she looked at his face and sort of lost that train of thought.

Oh, mercy.

How could anyone look that good at this time of day? Maybe it was the semidarkness, but Joelle didn't think so.

Dallas hadn't been practice for her, that's for sure.

He'd been her benchmark, and no man since had quite measured up. Maybe no one ever would. Not exactly a comforting thought for a woman who wanted marriage and kids.

She ran her hand between them. "You didn't have all this chest hair when you were seventeen." She liked it. A lot. Joelle tugged at some of the strands until he winced and opened one eye to peek out.

"Put your hand lower and do that, and I might wake up."

Now she chuckled, and her hand was already heading in that direction when a buzzing sound cut through the room. Both of them cursed, and Dallas leaned over her to pick up his cell, which was on the nightstand.

"It's Lindsey," he relayed, adding the exact profanity that Joelle was thinking. Dallas hesitated, as if he might not answer it at all, but then his attention went back to the clock.

Judging from the hour, this probably wasn't a casual call. Still leaning over her, Dallas hit the answer button, and without actually picking up the phone, he put the call on speaker. "What the hell is wrong now?" he greeted.

Joelle hoped that a miracle would happen and that Lindsey would say she had good news. That their names had been miraculously cleared. But Lindsey didn't answer at all. Not with words, anyway. The woman was sobbing.

Dallas rolled his eyes. "Okay, I'll bite. Why the tears?"

Lindsey said something, but Joelle couldn't make out what. The woman's sobs got worse.

"Lindsey?" Joelle tried. "You have to tell us what's wrong."

"It's Owen." Joelle heard that part loud and clear, but it took several more moments of loud crying for Lindsey to continue. "I went to his place, and he was packing. He was planning to run out on all of us. On me."

Dallas grumbled more profanity, got off the bed and started to dress. Joelle did the same, though the only thing she had in the room was her nightshirt. Still, she'd have to dress because it was apparent that Owen was about to skip bail.

"Did you call the sheriff or the marshals' office?" Dallas asked.

"No," Lindsey answered. "I shot him."

Dallas had been about to step into his jeans, but he froze. So did Joelle. "Who did you shoot?" he demanded.

"Owen." The sobs turned to hysterics now. "I shot him, and he might be dying."

Joelle looked at Dallas to see if he believed what Lindsey was saying. He apparently did. So did Joelle. It was possible that Lindsey was faking all the crying, but it seemed genuine. Plus she suspected that Lindsey wasn't exactly emotionally stable right now.

"Where are you?" Dallas asked. He continued to dress while he waited for Lindsey to answer.

"Owen's house in town. I didn't know what to do. Who to call."

"An ambulance would have been a good start," Dallas answered. "Hang up right now and call 911. Tell them exactly what you just told me."

"I will." She paused again, and Joelle could hear someone mumbling in the background. "You should come out here. Owen says he has some things to tell Joelle and you."

"What things?" Dallas demanded.

"Something about Jonah Webb's murder."

And with that, Lindsey ended the call. Hopefully so she would phone an ambulance. However, Dallas didn't trust her to do that because he motioned for Joelle to get dressed, and he made the call himself and then asked the dispatcher to give him an update on Owen's condition as soon as possible.

Joelle hurried, and she tried to focus just on getting dressed, but the thoughts racing through her head slowed her down. She had to consider that this was some sort of ruse by Lindsey. But what if it wasn't?

What if Owen really was dying?

After everything he'd done and tried to do to Dallas and to her, Joelle despised the man, but she truly hoped that Lindsey hadn't murdered him.

She was still dressing when Dallas appeared in the doorway. "I told Kirby's nurse what's going on. Harlan is walking over here now to stay with them while I'm gone. I'd like for you to stay here, too."

Harlan was Dallas's foster brother and a fellow marshal. A man she trusted as she did all his brothers. From what she'd learned in her background checks, he lived in a house on the grounds of the ranch, which meant it shouldn't take him long to arrive.

Joelle shook her head. "I want to go with you. I want to find out what's going on."

He gave her a flat look, then lifted his cell. "That's what phones are for."

Since he looked ready to leave without hearing her argument, Joelle caught his arm. "If Owen's alive, I'd like to hear what he has to say. By the time we get into town, he'll be at the hospital anyway."

"But I'll want to question Lindsey," he argued. "And I don't want you anywhere near her, especially if she tried to murder Owen."

"Fine." Joelle wasn't exactly thrilled to be near Lindsey, either. "Talk to her. You can do that after we see Owen and after the sheriff has taken her into custody."

She braced herself to continue the argument, but Dallas glanced at the time on his phone. The seconds were ticking away fast.

And Owen could be dying while they debated this.

Joelle wasn't sure the man had any revelations about Webb's killer, but at this point, he was their best shot at learning the truth. Because she was almost positive that Owen had either murdered Webb himself or else he knew the identity of the killer.

She heard another buzzing sound. Not Dallas's phone but rather the security system. Joelle hurriedly put on her shoes, the blasted heels that she intended to burn first chance she got, and raced after Dallas. By the time she made it to the front door, he had disarmed the security system and was letting Harlan inside.

Harlan shucked off his raincoat and Stetson, and his gaze lingered a moment on his brother before it came to her. Though he didn't smile, she thought he might be pleased to see her. It was always hard to tell with Harlan. He had a quiet intensity about him that could be a little unnerving.

"You're back?" Harlan asked her. Joelle followed his gaze down to her neck and wondered if there was a love bite there. Probably. Dallas knew it was her hot spot and the kisses had gotten pretty intense when they'd had sex. So, the *"you're back"* comment took on a whole new meaning, and Harlan likely wanted to know if she and Dallas were back together.

They weren't.

But Joelle didn't have time to get into that now.

"If you can, get me any updates on Owen and the evidence the CSIs pulled out of Rocky Creek," Dallas instructed Harlan. "And rearm the security system when we leave." He opened the door and did a lawman's surveillance of the front of the house.

"You expecting trouble?" Harlan asked him.

"I think it's already here."

That sent Harlan's gaze back to her again. Specifically, back to her neck. Joelle didn't address it but instead followed Dallas to his truck, which was parked at the edge of the porch steps. Good thing, too, because it was still raining. No lightning or thunder, thank God, but it was a slow, steady downpour.

Dallas didn't waste a moment getting her inside before he drove away, still keeping watch of the area. She looked, too, but when they were away from the house, she pulled down the visor and checked herself in the vanity mirror.

And there it was.

Definitely a love bite. Maybe two.

"Sorry," Dallas said, obviously noticing them, too.

She was about to say there was no need for an apology, that she'd gotten a lot of pleasure from those bites, and everything else he'd done to her in bed, but she didn't have time to answer.

"We'll talk later," he said. And he didn't sound very happy about that. Didn't look happy, either.

Of course he wasn't.

He was still trying to come to terms with the child they'd lost. With the secret she'd kept. One night of great sex wasn't going to undo all of that, but Joelle hoped it was a start.

However, she rethought that.

Maybe a start wasn't even possible. The sex had always been good between them. Still was. But sex alone wasn't going to heal their wounds.

That sent a jolt of pain through her heart. Mercy. Hadn't she learned to shield her heart any better than this?

Apparently not.

Because here she was falling hard all over again for Dallas.

His phone buzzed, and while the truck slogged down the gravel and dirt road, Dallas took the call on speaker.

"It's me, Clayton," he said. "The CSIs got that safe open."

Joelle certainly hadn't forgotten about the floor safe that the CSIs had found, but with everything else going on, she'd put it on the mental back burner.

"There was some cash in it," Clayton explained. "About five grand and a passport."

Joelle thought about that for a moment. "You think Webb was planning on leaving the country or something?"

"Maybe. There were also some account books that'll probably prove he was skimming money from the state."

Definitely not a surprise, but maybe the contents of the safe was just his getaway kit. Something he could grab in a hurry if he came under scrutiny.

Which was about to happen.

Because Kirby had been on the verge of launching a full-scale investigation. Of course, if they were to believe Sarah, Webb hadn't been concerned about that investigation because he'd already gotten approval to keep Rocky Creek open.

"One more thing," Clayton said. "Owen still hasn't produced the so-called real knife that he claims he received."

And with Owen hurt, maybe dead, it might take the marshals a while to find the knife or anything else Owen had hidden away. Not good. Because maybe if all the pieces of this case came to light, it would be better than keeping things hidden away.

While Joelle mulled that over, she felt a jolt of a different kind. A real one. Dallas must have hit a massive pothole or something, and the truck lurched forward so quickly that Joelle's head hit the ceiling.

"What the hell now?" Dallas growled.

He brought his truck to a jarring stop and threw open the door so he could look out. He immediately snapped back toward her, grabbed onto her and shoved her down on the seat.

Joelle didn't even have time to ask what was wrong before Dallas drew his gun.

DALLAS DIDN'T SEE ANYONE OUT there, but someone had to be. Someone with bad intentions, and he had the flat tires to prove it.

"What's happening?" Joelle asked.

Dallas pushed her lower onto the seat, covering her as best he could with his body, and he tried to pick through the darkness and the rain to see if he could spot anyone.

He didn't.

"Someone put a spike strip across the road," he explained. "The kind that cops use to flatten the tires of someone trying to escape."

"Oh, God," she whispered.

Yeah. That was basically his reaction, too.

Dallas wanted to hope for the best and believe this was some kind of prank, but his luck wasn't that good. Plus, coupled with Lindsey's call that had ultimately gotten them out of the house, he figured things could get ugly fast.

But had Lindsey orchestrated this? Whatever *this* was? He wouldn't put anything past the woman, not with her insane jealousy when it came to Owen. Of course, there were other immediate suspects who came to mind.

Rudy and Sarah.

Owen, too.

Because now that Dallas had time to think about it, Owen might not be shot. He might have been the one who put Lindsey up to doing this.

He reached in his pocket, grabbed his cell and handed it to Joelle. "Call Harlan and let him know someone just disabled my tires. Tell him what's going on but that I don't want him to come outside." Because this might be some kind of an attempt to get to Kirby. "Have him phone Clayton or Declan so they can drive out here."

It would take a while for either of them to arrive since they were both at the marshals' office in town. Calling Slade and Wyatt wouldn't speed things along, either, since both were out of the county on assignments.

Joelle made the call, and even though her voice was shaky, she gave Harlan the information.

"What now?" she asked, slipping the phone back into his pocket.

"We wait."

It wasn't the best of plans, sitting out on a ranch road in the dark. There were trees and fences. A lot of places for an attacker to hide. Still, the alternative was trying to get back to the house with his tires disabled. He could maybe do it, creeping along at a speed where anyone could catch them. But he didn't want to risk leading someone dangerous back to the house where Kirby was.

Of course, he might not have a choice.

He didn't want to put Joelle at further risk, either.

Because he was practically wrapped around Joelle, he could feel her tense muscles and knew she was scared. Over the past couple of days, she'd been put in too many positions like this, and he wanted to put an end to threats. Unfortunately, the only way to do that was to catch the person responsible.

Maybe the person who'd put down that strip to shred his tires.

The thought had no sooner crossed his mind when the movement caught his eye. At first he thought it was the motion of the wipers slashing across the windshield, but he had a closer look. Not the wipers.

There appeared to be someone ducked down behind the fence.

Even though the truck headlights were still on, they weren't aimed in the right direction for him to confirm his theory, and he definitely wasn't getting out and leaving Joelle alone. If Lindsey was behind this, it was exactly what she would want him to do so she'd stand a better chance of getting her hands on Joelle.

His phone buzzed, and Joelle took it out for him. "It's Harlan," she relayed in a whisper.

"Put it on speaker," Dallas instructed. He wanted to keep his hands free in case someone out there had bad intentions.

"Don't go to Owen's," Harlan immediately said. "I just got a call from the deputy who responded, and neither Lindsey nor Owen is there."

Hell. Dallas was hoping they were not only there but that both had been either arrested or contained in some sort of way.

"You need help where you are?" Harlan asked.

"No." Not yet, anyway. "Stay put. I don't want Kirby left alone. How long before the others get out here?"

"Twenty minutes maybe. The bottom part of Durham Road is flooded so they'll have to drive around."

Another complication he didn't need, but Dallas had no choice but to end the call and wait. If there was someone armed out there, he wanted backup.

"Maybe it's my imagination," Joelle whispered, "but I think I smell smoke."

Dallas lifted his head, sniffed. Yeah, there was a the faint smell of smoke, but he thought it might be lingering from what had happened the day before at Rocky Creek.

He looked out but didn't see any signs of fire or smoke, and even if there had been, the rain would have likely doused it. But the smell got stronger, and Dallas finally saw something he didn't want to see.

The wisps drifting up from beneath his truck.

"It's smoke," he confirmed.

Joelle automatically lifted her head to have a look, but he pushed her right back down. Dallas mumbled some profanity and inched closer to the side mirror so he could try to see what was going on. Still no flames, but he was getting a bad sense of déjà vu. Maybe the person who'd orchestrated that smoke at Rocky Creek had managed to do the same beneath his truck. Of course, it could be a real fire, too.

Either way, he had to move Joelle.

He couldn't wait twenty minutes for backup because they might be dead by then.

Since that shadow was on his side of the truck, Dallas figured they needed to go out Joelle's side. He reached across her and slightly cracked the door.

"I'll go first," he instructed, "and the second your feet hit the ground, I want us away from the truck."

She gave a shaky nod, and even though he could feel her fear, there was nothing he could do to lessen it right now. "Run where?" she asked.

There were several trees. Not good cover. But maybe they wouldn't need it. "Just stay next to me," Dallas said.

He crawled over her and used his shoulder to fully open the door. In the same motion, he caught her by the arm and helped her scramble from the truck. Dallas had already told her to hit the ground running, but they'd barely made it a step when a shot blasted through the air.

Joelle made a gasping sound, and both Dallas and she dived to the ground. It was like landing in a massive mud puddle, and he had to roll to the side and keep his gun lifted so that it wouldn't get wet.

"I'm Marshal Walker," he called out just in case this was a stray hunter.

But no such luck.

Another shot came right away, cracking through the rain, and this one slammed into the truck. Not the driver's side where he'd last seen that shadowy figure. No, this bullet tore into the back.

Dallas made a quick adjustment, slinging Joelle behind him so that he'd be between the shooter and her. It wasn't enough because from the sound of the shots, their attacker was using a rifle. A high-powered bullet could easily go through him and into Joelle.

Still, it was too risky to move.

Or maybe not.

The next shots weren't single rounds but three bullets that came back to back, and each of them smacked into the ground between the truck and them.

The shooter was moving. Getting closer. And that meant Dallas had to do something. He tried to pinpoint where he thought their attacker was, then he levered himself up and fired. He wasn't sure where his shot went, but it hadn't hit a person.

Joelle was shaking now. Probably a combination of the fear and the fact she was lying in cold, muddy water. Dallas was cold, too, but he tried to keep his hands steady, and he also tried to listen for the sound of any footsteps or movement.

He finally saw something.

The shadowy figure was back. Someone wearing dark clothes and moving from the side pasture and ducking into the trees that lined that part of the fence.

Another shot came at them.

But this time Dallas saw the person lift the rifle. Not an ordinary lift, either. Their attacker didn't even aim. He blindly shot toward them and kept moving. And he wasn't moving in a direction that Dallas wanted him to go.

The shooter was headed straight for the house.

Chapter Seventeen

Joelle felt every muscle in Dallas's body tense, and he cursed. Even though he had her pressed against the soggy ground, Joelle managed to lift her head enough so she could try to see what had caused his reaction.

She saw the blurry figure, cloaked in the rain and carrying a rifle. But the person was no longer shooting at them but rather making a beeline for the ranch house.

Where Kirby was.

Oh, mercy.

Kirby was much too weak to fight off an attacker. Yes, Harlan was there as well, but the shooter might fire into the house before Harlan even realized what was happening.

Dallas dug his heels into the mud so he could get to his feet, but he remained in a crouching position. He fired at the figure. The blast jolted through her, making her nerves even more raw than they already were.

However, whoever it was must have been expecting Dallas to shoot because the person ducked out of sight behind one of the trees.

"I have to go to the house," Dallas whispered. "And I have to take you with me." It was definitely an apology.

One that she didn't need.

Because Joelle was already getting to her feet, too.

Whoever this shooter was, she couldn't let Kirby become the target of an attack.

Dallas grabbed her wrist with his left hand and started leading her up the side of the road. The mud was so thick that her shoe got stuck in it, and she finally just stepped out of the heels and left them behind.

The rain spat at them, almost blinding them at times, and it didn't help that it was still practically pitch-black. The farther they moved from the truck headlights, the worse it got.

Ahead, she could see the spot where the shooter had disappeared, but she saw no movement to indicate he or she was still there.

He. Or. She.

She mentally repeated that. Because in the darkness, it had been impossible for her to tell if the shooter was male or female. It could be Lindsey or Sarah. Of course, it could also be Owen or Rudy. Whoever it was, the person clearly meant to do them or someone in the house harm.

She and Dallas seemed to be running at a snail's pace, mostly because of her. Joelle just couldn't keep up, and with every step she took, she landed in a deeper and deeper bog. It didn't help that the mud was now caked on her feet and legs because that only slowed her down more.

She caught another glimpse of movement. The person came out from cover for just a second before ducking back behind another tree. Definitely moving toward the ranch house.

But what did he or she want?

If it was one of their suspects, none of them had a beef with Kirby or Harlan. Well, not that Joelle knew of, anyway. Unless…

"Owen could try to hurt Kirby to get back at us," she blurted.

She hadn't meant to say that aloud, but it was clear from Dallas's reaction that he'd already considered it. Probably because Owen hadn't hesitated to hurt Dallas with the baby's birth certificate.

Dallas kept them moving, but so did the person ahead of them. Joelle figured they could catch up with this shooter, but they were nearing the point where catching up wouldn't help if the person fired that rifle into the house.

Behind them, she saw the slash of lights, and for a moment, Joelle thought the lightning had returned. But this light wasn't coming from the sky but rather the road, and it was the headlights of a vehicle. She prayed it was one of Dallas's brothers, but she was scared to the bone that it was help coming for the person who'd shot at them. After all, their attacker had hired those gunmen in the woods and could have called them back in to finish the job.

"Keep watch behind us," Dallas told her.

She did, allowing him to lead her along the edge of the road. "Can you still see the person with the rifle?"

"Yeah." And since that was all Dallas said, she figured that meant the person was still heading for the house.

Joelle pinned her attention to the headlights, watching them bounce over the watery road. She was breathing through her mouth now, waiting, and she saw the vehicle when it turned onto the road that would soon— very soon—take them to where Dallas had left his truck.

The lights slashed right in her eyes, blinding her, and Dallas yanked her out of the way. He pulled her into some shrubs that fronted a few massive oaks. The oaks were too far away to use for cover, but maybe the shrubs would protect them enough if there were gunmen in that vehicle.

Joelle stumbled, one of the thorny shrubs clawing at

her arm, and she had to hold on to Dallas to keep from falling. But somehow, he kept them moving.

Even over the slapping sound of the rain, she heard his phone buzz. Maybe it was one of his brothers letting him know they were the ones in that vehicle. Joelle reached for the phone to answer it, but then she heard another sound. Not buzzing. But footsteps, as if someone were running just to their left.

She turned in that direction just as someone grabbed her by the arm and jerked her violently toward them. If it hadn't been for the mud and her bare feet, she might have been able to keep her balance. But the motion caught her off guard and she went flying in the direction of the person who'd grabbed her.

Dallas snapped toward her and raised his weapon, but it was too late.

Someone jammed a gun against Joelle's back.

DALLAS'S HEART WENT TO HIS knees.

Hell.

This was exactly what he'd been trying to avoid, and here he'd let it happen right next to him. He'd had his attention so focused on the rifle-toting person ahead of them that he hadn't taken enough precautions to make sure the shooter was acting alone.

And now Dallas had proof that he wasn't.

Before someone had grabbed Joelle, he'd gotten a glimpse of the rifleman, and there was no way the guy could have doubled back and gotten to them this quickly.

So who was the SOB who now had Joelle locked in a chokehold? Judging from the guy's beefy arms, it wasn't one of their suspects.

His phone stopped buzzing, which meant the call had probably gone to voice mail. He already had too much to deal with right in front of him, but he prayed that the call hadn't been from Harlan to say that he and Kirby were under attack.

"You don't want to do this," Dallas tried. Yeah, it wasn't much of a threat, but he took aim in the general direction of the guy's head. The problem was that it was also in the direction of Joelle's head.

Dallas didn't have anything resembling a clean shot.

And that was just the first of his concerns. The guy was already dragging Joelle back, toward the trees, trying to take her God knows where. Plus there was a rifleman out there somewhere. And that vehicle. If his brothers weren't in there, then he and Joelle were in big trouble.

Still, Dallas wasn't just going to let this Neanderthal haul her away.

Even in the darkness he could see the fear all over Joelle's face. This guy outsized her by a lot, and he was obviously much stronger than she was. He was moving her as if she were a rag doll.

Trying to keep watch and listen for signs that someone else was sneaking up on them to join this, well, whatever this was, Dallas inched after the man and Joelle.

"Let her go," Dallas ordered. "If you want a hostage, then take me."

"Admirable," the man growled, "but I got my orders." He was wearing a small communicator looped over his ear, and he said something into it that Dallas didn't catch.

Probably talking to his boss.

Dallas intended to find out who that was and make the person and this lackey pay. Joelle had enough bad memories to last a lifetime without these jerks adding more.

"Dallas?" someone called out.

It was Clayton, and Dallas would have been relieved

at hearing his brother's voice if there hadn't been another sound.

A gunshot.

"Stay down!" Dallas shouted to Clayton, and he prayed he wasn't too late with that warning. "Someone with a rifle might be moving toward the house. Call Harlan if you can."

Might.

Dallas had to accept that the rifleman might have been a decoy. Someone to distract him so that someone else could go after Joelle.

And unfortunately that's exactly what'd happened.

But what the devil did this person want with Joelle?

Maybe it was Lindsey or Owen hell-bent on revenge. That would make sense. Well, it would in the minds of criminals and lunatics. Of course, this could be connected to the investigation. Which meant any of their suspects could have orchestrated this.

The question was, why?

Dallas slung off the rain from his face and eyes. It didn't help. More rain came, blurring his vision, and even though the sky was starting to lighten up, it was still hard for him to see much other than Joelle and those frightened eyes.

"What do you want from me?" Joelle managed to ask, despite the arm clamped around her throat.

The guy didn't answer. He just continued to move backward, dragging Joelle right along with him.

Dallas hadn't thought things could get much worse, but the man pushed aside one of the tree limbs and stepped back onto one of the many ranch trails that snaked through the property. Normally, there would have been nothing on this particular trail—it was used to move equipment in and out of the adjacent pasture.

But there was a truck parked there now.

Joelle's eyes widened when she spotted the vehicle, and she frantically started shaking her head. She didn't have to say it aloud, but Dallas knew if this man managed to get her into that truck, he would have a much better chance of escaping with her.

That couldn't happen.

Dallas moved forward and tried to figure out the best way to stop this. He couldn't lunge for Joelle because her captor had a gun aimed right at her. But obviously the guy hadn't wanted her dead or she already would be. He would have shot her rather than grab her.

That took Dallas's heart past his knees and to the ground. He couldn't lose Joelle. Not again and not like this.

"Whatever you want from her," Dallas bargained with the guy, "use me to get it instead. I'm sure Owen wants me dead anyway."

The guy didn't even react to that. He just kept backing up until he reached the truck.

Dallas waited, watched, because the man would have to reach behind him and open the door if he wanted to get Joelle inside the cab of the truck. For that to happen, he'd have to let go of the chokehold unless the moron was stupid enough to use his right hand, where he held the gun.

Either way, Dallas had to strike.

He readied himself to ram right into the guy, but Joelle's kidnapper didn't ease up on the chokehold and he darn sure didn't lower the gun.

Behind him, the truck door opened.

And Dallas saw the person inside.

Not behind the wheel, either. After opening the door, the person hurried back across the seat to the passenger's side where the darkness and the shadows were too murky for Dallas to make out any features. However, he could see the outline of a gun and it was pointed directly at him.

"You'll get a call in a few minutes," Joelle's captor said to Dallas. "You'll have a chance to save her if you do everything we say."

There was no safe shot for Dallas to take. Nothing he could do that wouldn't put Joelle in the direct line of fire. He could only watch as the man dragged her into the truck and slammed the door.

Chapter Eighteen

Everything happened so fast that Joelle didn't have time to fight back. The hulk of a man threw her into the truck and before she could even bring up her arm to try to slug him, someone else rammed another gun into her rib cage.

And that someone was Sarah Webb.

Joelle wasn't exactly surprised to see the woman. She wouldn't have been shocked to see any of their suspects, but knowing her captor's identity didn't explain why all of this was happening.

Dallas launched himself at the truck, trying to open the door to get to her, but her captor had already locked it. And he started the engine and sped away.

Joelle's heart was pounding now because they were clearly taking her to a secondary scene. Away from Dallas. Away from the ranch where his brothers might be able to help her get free.

She started thinking that she was about to die, but that wasn't nearly as terrifying as the thought of Dallas being killed. And that's exactly what she thought might happen when the driver calmly lifted his gun and fired.

Joelle heard herself scream because she thought he'd shot at Dallas, but she quickly realized he had fired overhead. The bullet slammed into the roof of the truck.

A warning shot.

Probably to get Dallas to back off.

He didn't. Dallas latched on to the door handle, but the driver gunned the engine and sped away. She saw Dallas flung to the side. As horrible as that was, at least he hadn't been shot. But Dallas didn't stay down. He jumped to his feet and starting running after them.

"He won't stop," Joelle mumbled, and she turned toward Sarah. "He won't stop until he has you behind bars."

"And that's why I have you," Sarah said. Not calmly, either. There was a high pitch to her voice. More than nerves. Her hand was shaking, too. Probably because she'd never done anything like this.

That only made the situation more dangerous.

Joelle didn't like her odds with a shaky kidnapper who wanted to do God knows what to her.

"I'm guessing this means you killed your husband," Joelle said, trying to keep an eye on the driver, Dallas and Sarah. The mud was slowing them down, but Dallas was quickly losing ground.

"You already knew that," Sarah insisted.

But Joelle hadn't. Not until now, and *now* seemed a little too late.

"You and Dallas put it all together." Sarah kept glancing back at Dallas, too. "And then you found the safe beneath the floor."

Joelle shook her head and nearly blurted out what exactly was in that safe, but she decided to go with a question instead. "What do you think the CSIs will find that will implicate you?"

"Too much." Sarah's mouth was shaking now. In fact, nearly every part of her was. "I threatened to kill him, and he said he'd recorded the threat. That he'd lock it away to give to the cops if I tried to do anything."

Joelle didn't tell her there wasn't a tape or anything

else that would incriminate the woman. She just waited, listening, and she prayed that she could figure out a way to stop all of this before Dallas got hurt.

"I need Dallas to destroy everything in that safe," Sarah continued. "As long as I have you, Dallas will do that. He'll do anything to protect you. I could see it in his eyes."

Yes, Dallas would indeed do anything to protect her, and that's what scared Joelle most. She could no longer see him on the trail behind the truck, but at the speed they were moving, he'd soon catch up. And the hired gun behind the wheel might try to shoot him even if it meant Sarah had to rely on someone else to destroy evidence she believed existed.

"You just couldn't leave it be, could you?" Sarah grumbled.

No. Not with the governor's inquiry and not with Dallas's prints on the knife. Of course, they now knew how the prints had gotten there.

"Why did you kill him?" Joelle asked. Not that she had a burning desire to know, but she wanted to keep Sarah talking while Joelle tried to come up with a way out of this.

"It was a bad day," Sarah answered. She kept her attention nailed to Joelle. "Jonah ordered me to get Declan from the infirmary, but he wasn't there. He'd sneaked out or something."

"Because Webb had beaten him," Joelle provided.

Anger flashed through Sarah's eyes. "Because he deserved it. That brat was always causing trouble, and he'd started a firestorm that day. When I told Jonah that Declan wasn't in the infirmary, he didn't believe me."

Joelle glanced behind them. Still no sign of Dallas. "Webb thought you were protecting Declan?"

"Yes!" Sarah said with a curse. "I wouldn't do that. Not for him, not for any of you. None of you ever lifted a finger to help my boy, Billy, when Jonah was beating on him."

"We were kids," Joelle reminded her.

"Kids having sex. You were all disgusting as far as I was concerned, and if Declan had been where he was supposed to be, I would have taken him to my husband's office."

For no doubt what would have been another beating.

"Jonah said if I didn't find Declan in five minutes he was going to give me what Declan was supposed to get." Sarah's mouth tightened. "I couldn't go through that again. So I pretended to look for the brat, but I put on some gloves and used the knife that I knew had Dallas's prints."

"You wanted to set Dallas up?" Joelle shook her head. "Why?"

"I didn't set him up. Well, not at first. I just wanted some insurance in case the cops pointed the finger at me. I locked the knife away, and the day they found Jonah's body, I sent the knife to Owen and told him to make up a story about how he got it."

So Owen had known for almost two months that Sarah had killed her husband. And yet he'd withheld that and instead implicated Dallas and had tried to force her into marriage. That shouldn't have surprised her, but Joelle felt even more disgusted with the man.

"Unlike the rest of you, Owen was always a good boy," Sarah concluded. Her gaze slashed to the driver. "Make sure everything's all right at the house, that he has Kirby by now."

Oh, mercy. "Why Kirby?" Joelle asked. "He's a sick man."

Sarah nodded. "And he's my insurance policy. If Dallas won't destroy that evidence for you, he'll do it for Kirby. At least he'd better. I used every penny of my savings to hire these two to help me."

So they were hired guns. Which meant they had nothing to lose. Sarah was paying them to do whatever she asked, even if meant sending Kirby to an early grave.

"You there?" the driver said into the ear communicator he was wearing, and he kept driving. Seconds later, he repeated his question.

Still no answer.

Good. Maybe that meant Harlan had stopped him.

Sarah cursed again. "He better not have failed," she snapped. And she jammed the gun harder against Joelle's ribs. So hard that it nearly knocked the breath out of her.

Clearly, the woman was working on a short fuse. Maybe even an unstable one. It was a risk—anything Joelle did at this point would be—but she was certain of one thing. Even if Dallas managed to destroy that evidence, Sarah wasn't going to let them live.

Dallas and she were the ultimate loose ends.

With that realization slicing through her, Joelle gathered all her strength and breath. She dug her feet into the floor to anchor herself. Then she slammed her entire weight into the driver.

Thankfully, he hadn't seen it coming. The steering wheel lurched to the left. So did the truck. And it flew off the trail right into the boggy ground. The jolt was instantaneous, as if they'd been in a collision. The truck jerked to a stop, tossing them forward into the dash and windshield.

The impact stunned her, and the pain shot through every part of her body. But she didn't let it stop her.

She pulled back and started fighting as if her life depended on it.

Because it did.

DALLAS RAN AS FAST AS HE COULD, battling both the rain and the mud. He had to get to Joelle, had to stop her from being taken away from the ranch. But he also couldn't risk another shot being fired. That's why he stayed off the trail, behind the trees and shrubs.

He had to believe that shot had been meant for him. He couldn't stand to think otherwise. No. He wouldn't go there. He would get to her and he would save her.

His brothers were somewhere on the grounds. Maybe one of them would be able to stop that truck before it reached the main road. Of course, that was a risk for them, too, but he knew without a doubt that each of them would take it to save Joelle's life.

Ahead of him, he heard the heavy thudding sound. And the scream. It was a woman's, but it didn't sound like Joelle. Still, that pushed him to pick up the pace, and when he threw back a low-hanging branch, Dallas spotted the truck sitting nose first in an irrigation ditch.

"Harlan has the other gunman!" Clayton shouted. He sounded close, but Dallas figured he was closer.

He hurried to the truck and threw open the first door he could reach—the one on the passenger's side. Two people came spilling out. Both of them fighting. Both yelling.

One of them was Joelle, thank God. Alive and okay, for the moment at least.

The other woman was Sarah. And she was fighting, too, but she had the advantage because she had a gun in her hand. Joelle had a death grip on the woman's wrist, but from what Dallas could tell Sarah's finger was still on the trigger.

Sarah's henchman, the driver, came scrambling across the cab of the truck and tried to latch on to Joelle. Dallas didn't let him do that. He rammed himself into the man, knocking him away from the fray.

Unfortunately, that took Dallas away from it, too.

From the corner of his eye, Dallas saw Clayton approach them. His brother had his gun aimed and ready, but he didn't shoot. Sarah and Joelle were practically wound around each other, and Dallas had no choice but to drag the gunman to the ground so he couldn't try to help his boss.

"Harlan has the other gunman in custody," Clayton called out. "And the guy's already squealing about a plea deal to testify against his boss, Sarah Webb."

Whether it was true or not, Dallas prayed that would make Sarah surrender.

It didn't.

The woman kept fighting, kept trying to aim that gun right at Joelle.

Enough was enough. Even though the hired gun outweighed Dallas and was probably a lot stronger, he didn't have the high stakes. He wasn't fighting for Joelle's life. Dallas rammed his elbow into the man's jaw and followed it by bashing his gun across his face.

Cursing and spitting blood, the man reared up to charge at Dallas, but before he could do that, the shot rang out. From the corner of his eye, Dallas saw that Clayton had put a bullet in the man's leg.

Dallas didn't take the time to see if that would stop the guy. Clayton had his back, but Clayton still didn't have a clean shot to stop Sarah. Praying it wasn't a mistake, Dallas launched himself toward the woman, hauling them both to the ground.

The shot was deafening.

It blasted through Dallas's head, and he could have sworn his heart, too. That's because the bullet hadn't hit him, and that meant it could have Joelle.

He heard himself shout out her name, but it sounded like an echo with the blast still ringing in his ears. Dallas latched on to an arm and gave it a fierce tug.

Joelle.

She was moving. Alive. But since she was coated in mud, he couldn't tell if she'd been wounded.

Sarah came up off the ground. "I won't let this happen!" she yelled. "I won't go to jail for killing that bastard."

And she pointed the gun right at Joelle.

Dallas still had hold of her arm, and he slung Joelle behind him. In the same motion, he aimed his own gun, praying that there wasn't too much water or mud in the barrel.

He fired.

And his shot slammed into Sarah's chest.

Unlike his brother, Dallas had to go for a kill shot. He couldn't risk Sarah pulling that trigger.

The woman froze, the gun slipping from her hand and onto the ground. Her stare was frozen, too, fixed on Dallas. She said something.

Three words.

Words that Dallas didn't catch because of the rain.

He didn't get a chance to ask her what she'd said because Sarah dropped to the ground right next to the gun she'd just tried to fire at them.

Clayton hurried closer to cuff the injured gunman, but Dallas's attention went straight to Joelle. He grabbed her, pulled her closer to make sure she hadn't been shot.

"I'm okay," she said, but her voice was as shaky as she was.

Dallas didn't take her word for it. He swiped away the mud and looked for any signs of injury. She had some cuts and scrapes on her face, and while it turned his stomach to see them, it was far better than the alternative.

Relieved, he pulled her into his arms. "I'm sorry." It was just one of the things he needed to say to her, but the others could wait.

"Sarah's alive," Clayton relayed to them, and he took out his phone and called for an ambulance.

Joelle pulled back and placed both hands on Dallas's face. "Did you hear her?"

Her voice wasn't just shaky now. It was pretty much frantic, and he wanted to dismiss it as part of the slam of adrenaline she was no doubt feeling.

But there was something else.

"Did you hear what Sarah said?" Joelle asked.

Dallas had to shake his head. Three words. But he hadn't heard. "What?"

Joelle moved closer to him and put her mouth right against his ear. He heard the shuddering sound her breath made. "Sarah said *I had help.*"

Chapter Nineteen

Dallas was tired of waiting. Joelle, his family and he had been through hell and back, and here he was waiting in his boss's office for his brother, Wyatt, to return with reports and updates. Yeah, he wanted to hear those, but he also wanted to get Joelle out of there and try to ease that worried look on her face.

They'd managed to shower off most of the mud and grime before Saul had ordered them all to the marshals' building so that Wyatt could brief them. But all of them—Harlan, Clayton and especially Joelle—looked ready to collapse. Dallas was sure he looked the same.

Dealing with adrenaline crash was always a bear.

Plus, there was all the other stuff going on. He'd shot a woman just hours earlier. It'd been a necessity, but that didn't make it easy to swallow. As if Joelle knew exactly what he was thinking, she reached out and slid her hand over his.

Their gazes met, and he saw a lot of emotion in her eyes. "Thank you," she whispered, "for saving my life again."

You're welcome didn't seem like the right thing to say. For that matter, neither did anything else he could come up with. He didn't dare tell her that it'd taken a dozen years off his life when he thought she'd been hurt. So instead of words that were pretty much useless, Dallas leaned over and kissed her.

Clayton made a sound of amusement. Harlan grunted.

Dallas ignored them and kissed Joelle anyway.

When he eased back, he saw a little heat mixed in with all the worry.

"I had help," Joelle said, repeating what she heard Sarah say. "What do you think Sarah meant?"

"You're sure you understood her correctly?" Dallas asked.

"She did," Clayton said. "I heard it, too."

Great. That was not the verification Dallas wanted. He needed this put to rest. Sarah had killed her abusive husband. End of story.

But maybe it wasn't.

"You believe Sarah had an accomplice?" Joelle's voice was tentative. Clearly, she didn't want that to be true, either.

"I don't know," Dallas said. But there were some things that didn't fit right in this. "According to the blood the CSIs found, it looks as if someone dragged Webb down a flight of stairs. And he was buried over a mile away from Rocky Creek."

"Webb was a big man," Clayton added. "It would have been next to impossible for a woman Sarah's size to do that all on her own."

"Next to impossible," Dallas repeated. "But still doable."

Maybe.

Harlan made a *hmm* sound that rumbled in his chest. "I'm thinking we shouldn't be borrowing trouble. Especially that kind of trouble."

Before Dallas or the others could agree with that,

Wyatt appeared in the doorway. "You all right?" he asked to no one in particular.

"We are now," Clayton mumbled. "Kirby, too."

Dallas was about to demand to know what was in those reports they were waiting on, but he frowned when his gaze landed on Wyatt.

Like Harlan, Wyatt was tall, around six-four, and right now he looked more than a little imposing since he had a busted lip, a butterfly bandage over a mean-looking cut above his eye, and blood all over the front of his shirt.

"*You* all right?" Dallas repeated, eyeing the blood. "I thought you were on prisoner transport duty before Saul called you back in to help with this Webb mess."

"I was. The prisoners didn't exactly cooperate. Don't worry, they look a lot worse than I do," Wyatt joked. And despite the busted lip, Wyatt flashed Joelle one of his killer smiles. "How about you? My brothers taking good care of you?"

She nodded, and her mouth quivered as she tried to return a smile, but it didn't quite happen. "We're just anxious to hear what's going on."

"Yeah, well, be prepared to hear a lot. Saul's still tied up with the locals, but he gave me the go-ahead to start things off." Wyatt sat on the edge of Saul's desk and added a *where do I start?* huff.

"All of you have been checked out by the medics, right?" he asked.

They nodded, one by one. Joelle and Dallas had some bruises, one particularly bad one on Joelle's right cheekbone that made Dallas want to punch the daylights out of the person who'd put it there. But he knew it could have been much worse.

"Saul's orders are that Dallas, Clayton and Harlan will take a few days of paid leave while he sorts through all this," Wyatt explained. "Declan, Slade and me will be on other duties out of the county. In other words, they don't want us within smelling distance of the wrap-up."

"You're still thinking we did something wrong?" Dallas asked.

Wyatt shook his head. "I'm thinking you did a lot of things right, including catching a killer. But there'll be a mess of paperwork. And Saul doesn't want anyone saying that any of you had a hand in giving it the right kind of spin to benefit Kirby or anyone else."

That wasn't an unreasonable request. Besides, Dallas didn't mind having a few days off to settle things with Joelle. He hoped that would mean coaxing her back to his bed. He'd been damn lucky to get her there the night before, but that luck might not hold.

"First of all, Sarah Webb isn't dead," Wyatt went on. "But she did go into cardiac arrest during surgery and is in a coma. The docs aren't sure if she'll come out of it, but things aren't looking good."

That punched at Dallas harder than he thought, and Joelle gave his hand another gentle squeeze. He'd never shot a woman before, and he prayed he never have to again.

"I understand Sarah confessed to her husband's murder before Dallas had to shoot her." Wyatt wasn't looking at them but rather the reports.

"Yeah," Dallas confirmed. "And she also confessed to trying to kidnap Joelle so she could force me to tamper with the evidence that the CSIs found. She thought there was something incriminating in the safe."

"There wasn't," Wyatt confirmed. "Not for her, anyway, but I'm sure Sarah did some other things to try to cover her tracks. Like setting up those trash cans so they'd spew smoke in the building where Joelle and you were conducting an investigation."

"An unauthorized one on your part," Saul said, coming to the doorway. Thankfully, he didn't elaborate on that.

"Sarah was going to have Kirby kidnapped, too," Joelle volunteered.

Yet another reason for him not to regret shooting Sarah. What a twisted woman to use a sick man to cover up her crimes.

Dallas looked around the room at the others to see if they were going to offer anything else. None of them said anything to Saul about what might have been a confession from Sarah before she collapsed.

I had help.

Hell, the woman had been bleeding out at the time she'd muttered those words so she might not have had a clue what she was saying. Judging from the others' silence, they were taking the same stance.

Wyatt put the one report aside and picked up another. "Owen was picked up the airport in San Antonio. He was trying to get on a flight to Mexico because he figured that was better than going to jail once Joelle testified against him."

"Which I would have done. And I'll still do it," she insisted.

Good. That would put Owen behind bars for a while. "You need to add charges for him drugging Joelle and trying to shoot us in the woods."

Wyatt shook his head. "That was Lindsey who did the drugging. Owen's not saying much, but she's been a regular little chatterbox. Can't shut her up, in fact. She wanted to stop the wedding, and that's why she drugged Joelle."

"And Lindsey sent those men after us?" Joelle asked.

"Nope. That was Sarah's doing. One of her hired guns—the one who Harlan nabbed outside the ranch house—is talking, too. Sarah hired the three guys to kidnap Joelle because she wanted to make sure Joelle married Owen."

"Owen?" Clayton and Dallas asked in unison.

Wyatt nodded, then shrugged. "It appears that Sarah was running scared when she thought Joelle's inquiry might lead to her arrest, and she wanted to help Owen force Joelle to marry him so that Owen in turn would help clear her name. If you hadn't carried Joelle out of the church when you did, then Sarah's men would have forced her to walk down the aisle."

His boss cocked his head and stared at Dallas over the top of his reading glasses. "Just to clarify—you did take Joelle out of that church because you were concerned about her safety, right?"

That was part of it, yeah. But he'd also done it so that she wouldn't release the report that he thought would incriminate Kirby.

"Yes," Joelle answered for him. "Dallas was protecting me."

"Good." Saul sounded a little skeptical. He cleared his throat and motioned for Wyatt to continue.

Wyatt went to the next report. "Owen agreed to turn over the real knife, the one that Sarah sent him, as part of a plea bargain his lawyers are trying to work out."

"It'll have my prints on it," Dallas reminded him.

"Figured that, but we have Rudy's statement that you picked up the knife in Webb's office. Then we have Sarah's confession that she used the same knife to kill her husband. That ties it up in a nice little package."

It did, and it was one less thing for Dallas to worry about. But the knife wasn't all that Owen had hidden away. "And what about the handkerchief with Kirby's DNA?"

Saul shrugged. "That could have come from anywhere

at any time. No chain of custody to make it credible to link Kirby to a crime. Especially considering that Sarah was more than willing to try to set up a marshal for a murder that she committed. It's not much of a stretch for her to try to frame Kirby, too, with his own handkerchief."

No. It wasn't a stretch, and Dallas wanted to keep it that way.

"Going back to the first attack in the woods," Joelle spoke up. "One of the gunmen said something, well, personal about me."

Dirty little secret. Dallas remembered that, and now he realized the gunman might have been referring to Joelle's pregnancy.

"Owen could have passed on any info that he had about you to Sarah," Dallas reminded her. And they already knew that Owen had the baby's birth certificate.

"Yes," she softly agreed, but he heard the anger mixed in with that softness. He was right there with her. He hated that Owen, and Sarah as well, had used their baby to try to get back at them.

"Anything I should know about this *personal* thing the gunman said?" Saul asked. "Didn't think so," he said a moment later when none of them spoke up.

Wyatt picked up the next report. "Rudy probably won't face any charges except for the stunt he pulled at Rocky Creek when he locked out the CSIs. We've got no proof, but we think Sarah might have been the one to take that shot at him in the woods. There's no love lost between those two."

"No," Clayton agreed. "And when Sarah realized she'd failed to rile up Rudy enough to destroy the evidence in Rocky Creek, she probably took her anger out on him."

Wyatt nodded. "That's my theory, too." He picked up yet another form. "And that brings us to Lindsey and her call about shooting Owen. She didn't. Sarah put her up to that by promising Lindsey that she'd help her get Owen back. Sarah talked Lindsey into making that call with the hopes of luring you and Joelle out to the house."

"And it worked," Joelle whispered.

What color she had in her face vanished. Well, except for that god-awful bruise. Dallas knew it would raise Saul's eyebrows, but he didn't give a flying fig about that. He leaned over and pulled Joelle to him.

She made a soft sound, and he heard the pain in it. Oh, yeah. It was going to take a while for her to start forgetting this.

Saul cleared this throat again. "The governor wants you to call him first chance you get," he said to Joelle.

She managed a shaky nod. A nod that didn't sit well with Dallas. Of course, she had to call her boss. And of course, the governor would want her back at work. But that would mean her leaving.

No.

That didn't sit well with him at all.

Her gaze came to Dallas's and he saw the tears shimmering in her eyes. A bad mix with the bruises, scrapes and his own worry and concerns.

"You were never practice," Dallas heard himself say.

And he said it a whole lot louder than he'd intended. Actually, it hadn't been a good time to say it at all, but he couldn't very well take it back. Especially since it was true.

Joelle blinked. Opened her mouth. Closed it. Then she looked around the room at the others.

"Could you excuse us a minute?" Dallas asked to no one in particular, but he didn't wait for an answer. He eased Joelle to her feet and got her out of there.

By the time they made it out into the hall and to Dallas's own office, there weren't any tears left in Joelle's eyes. But there was a Texas-size amount of confusion. He had a lot to tell her, and maybe what he said in the next few minutes would ease some of that confusion.

But she spoke before he could ease anything.

"You're sending me mixed signals, Dallas. One of the main reasons I left you was because you never asked me to stay. Heck, you never asked me to be your girlfriend. Or to even go on a date. You definitely never asked me to be…yours."

Yeah, and he was quickly coming to the realization that had been one of the biggest mistakes of his life. Dallas tried to figure out the best way to fix that, but after looking at Joelle, he decided to do what he thought was best. Heck, it might be the wrong thing to do, too, but it would make him feel a heck of a lot better.

Dallas pulled her into his arms, put his mouth on hers and kissed her.

She went stiff for a few seconds. Hopefully because she hadn't seen the kiss coming and not because she objected to it. Dallas deepened it just in case, and he finally heard the sound he'd been waiting for.

That little purr.

He been lucky enough to hear it the night before when they were in bed together, and it was music to his ears now. Music to his body when she sort of melted against him.

"You always did play dirty," she mumbled against his mouth.

Now, it was his turn to go stiff. Dallas eased back and met her gaze. "I'm afraid if you're thinking too clearly, you'll leave again."

She tilted her head to the side and stared at him. "You think the only reason I'll stay is if you keep me hot? Well, here's a news flash. Looking at you gets me hot. So technically, I never think clearly around you."

"Looking at me gets you hot?" he asked and tried not to smile. Heck, he failed at that, too.

She pushed her fingers against that smile. Frowned. And then moved her fingers so she could kiss him right back. But she didn't just kiss him. Joelle could play dirty, too, and she slid her body right against his.

In all the right places.

The kissing and touching were so good that Dallas wanted to haul her onto his desk and do things to her that he'd never considered doing in his office.

Later, he might.

But for now, he obviously had to finish that explanation.

Hard to do, though, with Joelle nibbling at his mouth and sliding her hand down his chest.

"Will you go on a date with me?" he asked.

Her mouth moved into a slow smile. She nodded. "I'd love to."

That was a good start, so Dallas went through the list of grievances she'd spelled out for him a few moments earlier. Except this one was a lot bigger than a date.

"I'm also asking you to stay," he tossed out there. "If that's not possible, then I can see about getting a transfer to Austin—"

She shoved her fingers against his mouth again. "You're asking me to stay? Here? In Maverick Springs?"

He moved her fingers so he could answer. "Yeah. I know it's not Austin, but—"

"I want to stay," she interrupted.

"You do?" Dallas tried not to sound too surprised, but he was. He'd expected to have to argue that point.

She nodded. Kissed him again in that idle way that

only Joelle and a siren could have managed. "Maybe I can open a law practice. I figure you owe me a lot of dates, and that's the way to collect on them."

"Good move." He liked the way she thought. The way she kissed. The way she touched.

Hell. He liked everything about Joelle. Always had. And that's why he moved on to the next item on his mental list.

"Sixteen years ago I should have asked you to be my girlfriend. Or go steady. I should have asked," he said.

Aw, heck. The tears popped back into her eyes, and he had a moment of panic that he'd blown it. But then she went sliding back into his arms and kissed him. It was hot, needy and everything he'd come to expect from a Joelle kiss. He wanted to get caught up in it. Caught up in her.

On his desk, since it was close and convenient.

But sex was going to have to wait.

Something he thought he'd never hear himself say when it came to Joelle.

"One more thing." Dallas looked her straight in the eyes. "I'm asking you to marry me."

She sucked in her breath so fast that she coughed. *Oh, man.* Obviously, Joelle hadn't seen that coming, and he was about to launch into the most important argument of his life to convince her why she should say yes.

"Yes," Joelle blurted out before he could argue. But then she shook her head. "Wait."

"You can't take it back." And he played dirty again and kissed her until neither of them had any breath left.

She pulled back, gasping a little. "I don't want to take my yes back. I just want to know why you're asking."

Oh. He got it then. She wanted the words. The ones

he'd been too young and stupid to give her sixteen years ago.

"I'm in love with you, Joelle."

Tears again, but he was pretty sure these meant everything was okay, that she wasn't taking back her *yes*.

"Good. Because I'm in love with you, too."

Dallas hadn't expected those words to go through him with the heat and intensity of Joelle's kisses. But they did. In fact, the words did more than that. They warmed him. They soothed him.

They made him happy.

And before now, before this moment, he wasn't sure he ever had been. Not completely. Not like this. That feeling slid through him. A feeling that he figured he'd get to experience for a long time. As long as Joelle was with him.

"You were never practice," he whispered to her.

She blinked. Shook her head. "Then what was I?"

"The same thing you are now. Joelle, you're the love of my life."

And to prove it, Dallas pulled her to him and kissed her again.

* * * * *

USA TODAY bestselling author Delores Fossen's new miniseries, The Marshals of Maverick County, is just getting started.
Don't miss ONE NIGHT STANDOFF, coming next month, wherever Harlequin Intrigue books are sold!

COMING NEXT MONTH from Harlequin® Intrigue®
AVAILABLE MAY 21, 2013

#1425 ONE NIGHT STANDOFF
The Marshals of Maverick County
Delores Fossen

Marshal Clayton Caldwell and Lenora Whitaker never knew their one-night stand would leave her pregnant and in the crosshairs of a killer.

#1426 TRUMPED UP CHARGES
Big "D" Dads: The Daltons
Joanna Wayne

When Adam Dalton's daughters are abducted before he's ever had a chance to meet them, this marine's will of iron won't let him give up until they are all a family at last.

#1427 ASSUMED IDENTITY
The Precinct: Task Force
Julie Miller

Jake Lonergan can't remember his past. But when single mom Robin Carter is threatened, he will put his life on the line to give them a future together.

#1428 MURDER IN THE SMOKIES
Bitterwood P.D.
Paula Graves

Security expert Sutton Calhoun is back in town, looking for a killer. When his investigation reunites him with the woman he'd left behind, will he also solve the mysteries of his own heart?

#1429 THE BEST MAN TO TRUST
Sutton Hall Weddings
Kerry Connor

Tom Campbell, the best man, is the only person wedding planner Meredith Sutton can rely on when a killer begins targeting a snowbound wedding party at Sutton Hall.

#1430 UNDERCOVER TEXAS
Robin Perini

A brilliant scientist wanted by international terrorists. A black ops soldier with too many secrets. The only way he can protect her and the one-year-old son he's never even held is to kidnap them.

You can find more information on upcoming Harlequin® titles, free excerpts and more at www.Harlequin.com.

HICNM0513

REQUEST YOUR FREE BOOKS!
2 FREE NOVELS PLUS 2 FREE GIFTS!

HARLEQUIN®

INTRIGUE®

BREATHTAKING ROMANTIC SUSPENSE

YES! Please send me 2 FREE Harlequin Intrigue® novels and my 2 FREE gifts (gifts are worth about $10). After receiving them, if I don't wish to receive any more books, I can return the shipping statement marked "cancel." If I don't cancel, I will receive 6 brand-new novels every month and be billed just $4.74 per book in the U.S. or $5.24 per book in Canada. That's a savings of at least 14% off the cover price! It's quite a bargain! Shipping and handling is just 50¢ per book in the U.S. and 75¢ per book in Canada.* I understand that accepting the 2 free books and gifts places me under no obligation to buy anything. I can always return a shipment and cancel at any time. Even if I never buy another book, the two free books and gifts are mine to keep forever.

182/382 HDN F42N

Name	(PLEASE PRINT)	
Address		Apt. #
City	State/Prov.	Zip/Postal Code

Signature (if under 18, a parent or guardian must sign)

Mail to the **Harlequin® Reader Service:**
IN U.S.A.: P.O. Box 1867, Buffalo, NY 14240-1867
IN CANADA: P.O. Box 609, Fort Erie, Ontario L2A 5X3
Are you a subscriber to Harlequin Intrigue books
and want to receive the larger-print edition?
Call 1-800-873-8635 or visit www.ReaderService.com.

* Terms and prices subject to change without notice. Prices do not include applicable taxes. Sales tax applicable in N.Y. Canadian residents will be charged applicable taxes. Offer not valid in Quebec. This offer is limited to one order per household. Not valid for current subscribers to Harlequin Intrigue books. All orders subject to credit approval. Credit or debit balances in a customer's account(s) may be offset by any other outstanding balance owed by or to the customer. Please allow 4 to 6 weeks for delivery. Offer available while quantities last.

Your Privacy—The Harlequin® Reader Service is committed to protecting your privacy. Our Privacy Policy is available online at www.ReaderService.com or upon request from the Harlequin Reader Service.

We make a portion of our mailing list available to reputable third parties that offer products we believe may interest you. If you prefer that we not exchange your name with third parties, or if you wish to clarify or modify your communication preferences, please visit us at www.ReaderService.com/consumerschoice or write to us at Harlequin Reader Service Preference Service, P.O. Box 9062, Buffalo, NY 14269. Include your complete name and address.

HI13R

MURDER IN THE SMOKIES
by
Paula Graves

When a string of murders rocks the small town of Bitterwood, Detective Ivy Hawkins's gut tells her they are all somehow connected. But no one believes her...except for Sutton Calhoun, a man Ivy would much rather forget.

Ivy closed the distance between them with deliberate steps. "I thought you swore you'd never let the dust of Bitterwood touch your feet again."

"That's a little melodramatic." Sutton laughed.

She shrugged. "You said it, not me."

True, he *had* said it. And meant it. And if Stephen Billings hadn't walked into Cooper Security two weeks ago looking for help investigating his sister's murder, he probably would've kept that vow without another thought.

He'd let himself forget Ivy and her uncomplicated friendship. And if her cool gaze meant anything, whatever connection they'd shared fourteen years ago was clearly dead and gone.

"I'm here on a job." He kept it vague.

"What kind of job?"

He should have known vague wouldn't work with a little bulldog like Ivy Hawkins. She'd never been one to take no for an answer. Maybe the truth was his best option.

"I'm here to look into a murder that happened here in Bitterwood a little over a month ago."

"April Billings," she said immediately.

He nodded. "Were you on that case?"

She shook her head. "She was the first."

Something about her tone tweaked his curiosity. "The first?"

"Murder," she said faintly. "First stranger murder in Bitterwood in twenty years."

"And you're sure it was a stranger murder?"

Her eyes met his, sharp and cautious. "All the signs were there."

"I thought you didn't investigate it."

"I didn't investigate it at the time it happened."

"But you've looked into her death since?"

She cocked her head slightly. "Who sent you to investigate this case? Are you with the TBI?"

He almost laughed at that thought. His father had had enough run-ins with the Tennessee Bureau of Investigation that both their faces were probably plastered to the Knoxville field office's front wall, right there with all the other most wanted. "No. Private investigation."

"You're a P.I.?" Her eyebrows arched over skeptical eyes.

"Sort of."

She was making him feel like a suspect. He didn't like it one bit.

Will Ivy and Sutton find the killer before
they become his next victims? Find out when
MURDER IN THE SMOKIES
hits shelves in June 2013, only from Harlequin Intrigue!

INTRIGUE

WHEN A MOTHER'S LOVE MEETS A FATHER'S INSTINCT...

Ex-marine Adam Dalton once dreamed of a life with
Hadley O'Sullivan, but war and a near-fatal injury cost
him dearly. Now he returns to Dallas to discover
the unthinkable—Hadley is the prime suspect in the
disappearance of her twin baby girls…the daughters
he hadn't known he had. Despite their past, Adam and
Hadley know finding their children is their only hope to
finally becoming a family—if time doesn't run out first.

TRUMPED UP CHARGES

BY JOANNA WAYNE

Available May 21 from Harlequin® Intrigue®.

HI69693

HARLEQUIN®
INTRIGUE®

SCARRED INSIDE AND OUT BY A PAST HE CAN'T REMEMBER...

Jake Lonergan can't remember his past and doesn't know if he's a heroic undercover DEA agent or the hit man who killed him and assumed his identity. He's determined to remain in the shadows, but when gorgeous single mom Robin Carter is attacked, Jake comes to her rescue...and finds it impossible to walk away from this fragile little family. Can he prove he's the good guy Robin is convinced he must be?

FIND OUT IN

ASSUMED IDENTITY

BY *USA TODAY* BESTSELLING AUTHOR
JULIE MILLER

Available May 21 from Harlequin® Intrigue®.

HARLEQUIN®

A Romance FOR EVERY MOOD™

**Stay up-to-date on all your
romance-reading news with the
Harlequin Shopping Guide,
featuring bestselling authors, exciting new
miniseries, books to watch and more!**

The newest issue will be delivered right to you
with our compliments! There are 4 each year.

Signing up is easy.

EMAIL

ShoppingGuide@Harlequin.ca

WRITE TO US

HARLEQUIN BOOKS
Attention: Customer Service Department
P.O. Box 9057, Buffalo, NY 14269-9057

OR PHONE

1-800-873-8635 in the United States
1-888-343-9777 in Canada

Please allow 4-6 weeks for delivery of the first issue by mail.